Singleton

by

Tony Myers

Singleton

www.tonymyers.net

Acknowledgments

I want to show my gratitude to a number of people who made this book possible. Without them, this book would not be what it is today. Thank you, guys! I appreciate all you did.

I would like to start by saying thank you to Dave and Karen Wilson. Dave, thank you for your encouragement and accountability in writing. I also appreciate you helping to push me to finish this book. Karen, thank you for your editing services. I know you spent many hours on the manuscript and for that I am extremely grateful.

Amy Sharp and the whole Sharp family also receive a large amount of my gratitude for their help with adoption research. You guys are great. You are to be greatly admired for your ministry and love of young ones. Keep up the good work!

Where would I be without my family? I want to thank both my immediate and extended family. Y'all were inspiring and encouraging. I appreciate all the excitement and interest in the book. I especially want to mention Charity, Hannah Beth, and Anthony. I love you guys so much!

Lastly, I would like to give my love and gratitude to God. Thank you for writing the greatest story ever told in your Son. I am forever grateful that He is writing that story on my heart. To Him be all glory, honor, and praise!

♋

To my family,

Thank you for the sacrifices you made to make this possible.

♋

Prologue

Henry was awakened by his wife who was in a near panic. She had heard a commotion in their basement and was worried. Someone might have broken into the house. They lived on a farm a couple of miles away from town, far from any of the main roads. Their children were now grown and had been gone for a few years; their home was typically quiet.

Henry was startled, "What is it, Dear?"

"I think someone has broken into our basement," his wife said, clearly shaking with fear.

Henry quickly got up and grabbed his shotgun from the closet. He went ahead and loaded a couple of shells as he left the room, still in his pajamas. He walked to the basement door. Taking a key out of his pocket, he unlocked the door.

As he opened the door he looked down the steps. It was dark. He couldn't see a thing.

He pointed the gun down the steps and descended. It was an old house and the steps creaked as he walked. The basement was a simple apartment, mainly just three rooms: a living area, a bedroom, and a bathroom. He reached the bottom and noticed he was sweating. Looking to his left, he saw glass shards scattered on the floor. There was a small window located at the top of the wall near the outside ground line. It had been smashed, and some of the furniture was stacked under it. Someone had used the furniture to climb back out of the window.

Henry knew an intruder had come in from the outside and he knew what that person was looking for. Quickly looking around the basement he saw that it was gone. The Resistance had come and struck. It had stolen from him. He felt light headed. He put the gun down.

The Master was going to be so upset. Henry didn't know whom he feared more, his leader or The Resistance. Sitting down on a nearby chair he called out to his wife, "Martha, I need you!"

Chapter 1

Jack Avery's eyes drifted slightly to the left as he drove over the Mississippi River entering Illinois, ready to start his new life. He was a long way from his home in Denver. It was early, and driving into the sun was a little uncomfortable in the first place. Their station wagon was full of boxes and they were pulling a large U-Haul trailer. The vehicle was silent, no conversation, no radio playing; the fan was off. It was silent.

His wife, Melissa, sat staring somewhat aimlessly out of the right side of the car, taking in the trip but also ready to get it over with. The trip across Nebraska and Iowa did not bear much in the way of scenery, but this didn't matter. Melissa was content with the silence.

Their relationship had been quite strained the past few years and as a result they didn't talk much. It seemed to

Jack they had been interacting more like business partners rather than lovers.

They had started out very much in love. Even before they were married, Jack felt that Melissa was always very aggressive in pursuing him. He knew this was kind of backward, but he really liked Melissa. They first met through a local dating website for Broncos fans. She was new to the Denver area and was looking for companionship. From their first date they seemed to really hit it off. This was, of course, to Jack's delight. He had always seen himself as an average guy: six feet tall, a hundred and eighty pounds, thin with slight athletic build; overall just average. He wasn't the type of guy at whom girls were throwing themselves, and because of this he was even more thrilled that he landed a girl like Melissa.

To Jack she was perfect. From the first time he saw her he was smitten by her beauty. Her dark brown hair was the perfect length—right past her shoulders. Her slim figure and short height were so pleasantly attractive. Anyone could see she was a true beauty. She was also very pleasant to be around. She had a very bubbly personality, and always seemed to be smiling and joking. When Jack planned their dates, he never had to plan very extravagantly to please her. She liked almost anything. Their favorite thing was an occasional round of mini-golf. Of course they never made it through a whole game, they always spent too much time laughing at bad shots and trying to make dramatic holes-in-one. From Jack's perspective it was a match made in heaven.

This all changed over the last couple of years. Melissa had suddenly gone cold toward Jack, not wanting anything to do with him. The change seemed to happen overnight. It was almost as though someone had flipped a switch in her mind, telling her that she didn't love him anymore. He had no idea what happened. It seemed as if she did not want to be married to him any longer.

At one point Jack thought she may be having an affair. He tried monitoring her phone calls and secretly looking through her personal items, but he found nothing. No strange phone calls, mostly just calls to her father. There were no strange items or gifts; he even recognized all her pieces of jewelry. At his most desperate point he hired a private investigator to follow her on days she went into the city, but even this turned up empty. He knew she was distancing herself from him and intentionally not wanting to do things with the family.

It was true they had a family now. Three years ago they adopted their daughter Olivia at nine-years-old. Jack and Melissa had always wanted a family, but Melissa felt she was too old to have a baby. They had only been married for six years. Jack was thirty-three at the time. Melissa was a couple of years older at thirty-five. He had always encouraged Melissa that a baby would be fun, and that having a child would keep them young. Melissa never gave in, never compromised—she had always wanted to adopt, and not just any child, but an older one. Melissa didn't think she would be able to handle a baby.

Under Melissa's demands they had been going through the adoption process since the beginning of their marriage. She convinced Jack that the process would take a while, and they had better start right away.

It took a couple of years before they settled on a little girl named Olivia. She was a strong little nine-year-old who never seemed to meet a stranger, and had an adventurous spirit about her. She was a fiery red-headed girl with slightly fair skin. She was so proud of her long red hair, and was always anxious to show it off.

To anyone on the outside it would be quite clear that she was adopted. Both her father and her mother had darker toned skin, along with dark hair. In many ways Olivia stood out like a sore thumb in the family, not looking remotely like either parent.

Olivia took to the family right away, accepting both Melissa and Jack as her new mother and father. She loved them both dearly, but her adventurous personality made her want to be with her father. Her teachers and her peers considered her a tom-boy. Some of her favorite activities included climbing trees, exploring the woods, playing baseball, fishing, playing with worms and insects, and just getting dirty.

She was also very inquisitive, always asking about anything imaginable. She took everything in. She learned a wide variety of different skills: from camping and backpacking, water safety, and food preparation to small construction skills and simple auto mechanics. Each new skill seemed to make her more independent, and from the day they adopted her Jack felt that she was growing up too fast. It was almost like she knew that she had to grow up quickly, and that she was preparing herself for something she may face in the future.

Jack always felt that something else was odd about Olivia, that there was some sort of secret surrounding her life. Not a secret in the sense that Olivia was hiding something from him, but rather a mystery to her life. Jack didn't know exactly how to explain it but it always left him feeling like he only knew half of his daughter. Most of the time he just shrugged off his feelings, attributing them to the fact that she was adopted at the age of nine.

He didn't know much of her past life. As an infant she was taken to a small children's home run by nuns. A young man, probably in his early twenties, just dropped her off. Even to this day the nuns who run the children's home do not know anything about the man. They say the man came in and right away put her in the arms of one of the nuns. He seemed to be in a hurry. He only signed about half of the necessary paperwork before leaving. They found out later that most of the information given seemed to be forged. The man was obviously trying to hide the identity of the child, and covering up any information regarding her background. He didn't even tell the nuns the child's name.

One of the nuns who took exceptional care of infants gave her the name Olivia, noting that if she were ever to have a little girl, Olivia would be her name. Of course, as a nun, this was probably as close as she would ever come to having a little girl of her own. The name started out unofficially, but over time it stuck, and before long all the nuns called the baby Olivia.

The nuns absolutely loved the girl. Olivia stayed with them in St. Thomas' Children's Home for the first nine years of her life before she was adopted. The incomplete and forged paperwork resulted in numerous court hearings from the state. It was as if the man who brought Olivia in consciously signed the paperwork in such a way that would frustrate and confuse state social workers. By the time everything was sorted out Olivia was a little girl who identified the nuns as her family. They took great care of her and saw it as a privilege to care for her until the day she was adopted.

The Avery family drove across the bridge spanning the Mississippi River, entering Illinois. Olivia slept soundly in the backseat of their '99 station wagon.

♋

Jack thought back to their last camping trip in Colorado. He and Olivia were backpacking in an area outside of Colorado Springs. It was their first night on the trip and Jack was frustrated with himself for forgetting one of the pivotal poles for their two-person tent. He was trying to use a stick to hold up one of the ends but so far it wasn't working. He cursed under his breath.

Meanwhile, Olivia was lying on her back, star gazing. It was a beautiful night and she was having a great time. The grass where she was lying felt cool, the wind blew gently, and they had made a large fire that was giving off just the perfect amount of heat at the moment. Olivia would have been content to sleep outside, but Jack, being cautious, thought there was a possibility of rain later in the night and he would rather not wake up soaked.

Olivia spoke up, "Daddy, isn't the sky just wonderful tonight? I can't remember a night when the stars looked as bright as they do tonight. You ought to come see."

"Not right now, Honey, I'm trying to get this stupid tent set up. I can't believe one of these poles is not here." Jack was beyond frustrated at this point. He wanted this trip to be perfect and so far just setting up the tent was giving him a headache.

"Like you always tell me, take a little break and then go back to it," Olivia said calmly. This was something Jack had said over the past three years when she became frustrated with a project. Even though he wanted to finish getting it set up, he knew she was right. A little break would be good for him. He got off his knees and walked over to where Olivia was lying and sat down beside her.

"Daddy, I know this is our last trip before we move, so do you mind if we do something extra special?"

"Sure, maybe, what are you thinking?"

"Would it ok if we slept out under the stars tonight? It's just so beautiful out here and I don't want to miss one second of it."

At first Jack did not like this request, but when he looked over at the tent that he had already spent more than enough time on, he decided to give in, "Why not! Let's do it. Who needs that old tent?" He felt relieved instantly.

"Thank you, thank you, thank you Daddy," Olivia said, rolling onto her side to give her father a hug.

They took some time to silently star gaze. One could not have asked for a better night of camping. Even though Jack was still a little worried, the idea of rain now seemed like a distant threat. He decided to take this quiet moment to talk to Olivia about their upcoming move.

"Olivia?"

"Yes, Daddy?"

"How do you feel about the move?"

Olivia thought for a moment, "Daddy, I think it will be fun to see a new place. I will miss it here, but you think we will still go fishing and do all the stuff we like to do?"

"Of course, Olivia, I don't want to ever miss any moments like this. You're my daughter and we are always going to have trips like this. Even when you grow up and if you have kids someday then we can take them along too."

"Yeah, thanks, Daddy. I love you." Olivia said quietly.

"I love you too," Jack responded.

They sat in silence for another few minutes when Olivia decided to speak up again, "Dad, I feel like, you know, we'll always be all right as long as we have these stars to look at."

"I sort of feel the same way."

Olivia continued on, "It's like when you see things like this it just makes you think of nice things, like how much God loves you and things like that."

Jack couldn't help but chuckle at how philosophical Olivia got on nights like this. He decided to throw in his two cents, "I know, Sweetie. I think it is just something where you wish everyone could see this sight. Like maybe the world would be a better place if everyone could just see what we see."

"Yeah, you're right, Daddy." Olivia was greatly enjoying the moment, "Think about this too, wherever you are around the world you can look up at the stars and probably be looking at the same star as someone a thousand miles away."

Jack nodded his head in agreement. "Yes, everyone we've ever met looks at the same stars and the people we'll meet later in life are maybe looking at the same stars now." Jack thought for a moment before continuing on, "Olivia, this is something we can always have. No matter how many miles apart we are from one another, we can always look up and see the same stars. It's like we can always be close to each other no matter how far apart we are."

Jack felt more relaxed than he had in a long time. The pressures of life had really gotten to him lately and many of his friends and coworkers said he seemed very up-tight. This was exactly what he needed, just a night to not worry about anything. The struggles in his marriage and demands of the upcoming move seemed so far away. He wished this moment would last forever.

"Daddy, I think this might be the best camping trip we've ever had."

"I hope so, Dear, as long as it doesn't rain," Jack said with a smile. Olivia couldn't help but burst out with laughter at this comment. It wasn't that it was very funny, but rather the late evening mixed with the irony of the comment in the midst of the serious conversation made her laugh.

"All right, Olivia, why don't we get some shut eye and start fresh in the morning?" Jack said.

"Sounds good, Daddy!"

It didn't rain.

Chapter 2

Coming off the bridge, Jack noticed they were low on gas. They had driven about an hour that day, and had one more to go. Without saying a word he exited right and headed for the gas station positioned right off the interstate.

"You should have filled up this morning as we were getting on the road. I want to get there as soon as possible," Melissa said agitatedly.

"Sorry, I just didn't think about it at the time. I was anxious to get on the road. I didn't think we were on any sort of time schedule," explained Jack.

Pulling into the station, he stopped at the middle pump on the store side. The station was not very busy as it was a Saturday. Melissa got out in a hurry, before Jack could even put the car in park. Her frustration was a regular these days. This morning Jack thought it might be attributed in part to the amount of coffee she had at breakfast.

As Jack was getting out his wallet, he looked in the rearview mirror to see Olivia stretching from her cramped sleeping position. She had stayed up a little longer than usual the night before. They had stopped overnight in Dubuque to see Jack's Uncle Frank, whom Olivia greatly loved. He always seemed excited to see her and could easily make her laugh.

"Good morning, Sunshine," Jack said in jest. Olivia was never a morning person, and didn't seem to really wake up until mid-morning. This sometimes caused little problems at school. "You were sleeping so soundly I didn't think you would even wake up when we stopped."

"Daddy, could I get something from the store," Olivia asked through a half-yawn.

"Sure, Honey."

Jack trusted Olivia to take care of herself. Even though she was only twelve, she was one of the most self-reliant people Jack had ever met. He never seemed to worry about her.

She opened the door and got out slowly. The summer air felt great. She stretched and yawned again before approaching the store. By this time Melissa was long out of sight into the store, probably in the ladies room.

There wasn't much to see in western Illinois, and this station fit the image. It had six pumping stations, all of which still had the mechanical numbers on the pumps as opposed to the digital. Jack grabbed the nozzle and began pumping the gas. He missed Colorado already! He had lived all his life in the Denver area. He had lived on practically every side of the town. He loved it all. He would miss the people. Over the years he had come to know so many folks around town that he could easily find help with nearly any problem he might be facing. It seemed like wherever he went he was always bumping into people he knew, and many times he was approached by people he didn't know. He was often mistaken for his younger brother, Steve, who greatly resembled Jack.

Click! The pump stopped. He took the nozzle out of the tank and put it back on the pump. The pump was so old that he would have to enter the store to pay.

Approaching the store, Jack found Olivia in one of her normal situations, talking to a stranger. An old man was seated on a porch area at the station, overalls on and cane in hand. It appeared that Olivia was describing to this man, in great detail, how to clean a fish. Olivia, in her naivety, did not realize that this old timer had probably cleaned more fish than she had seen in her lifetime. He was obviously very patient with her.

"Sir, is she bothering you?" asked Jack as he walked past, grabbing the entry door.

"No, Sir, this is very insightful stuff. I think I'm learning from a real pro here," the old man said, winking at Jack.

"Thanks," said Jack with an obvious eye roll, entering the store.

It was a basic gas station, a few snacks, drinks, souvenirs, and some overpriced groceries. Jack nodded briefly to the cashier before walking over to find the sunflower seeds. Even though it was early, Jack felt he needed something to make up for the lack of conversation on the trip. Grabbing a small bag, he headed over to the counter.

"Gas on number four, and these," he said, sliding the seeds over to the man behind the counter.

Looking out the window, Jack could see Melissa yelling at Olivia beside the car. She was angry with Olivia for speaking with the old man outside. Melissa had always reprimanded Olivia for talking with strangers. Jack was never too concerned, especially knowing that Olivia seemed to possess good judgment in knowing who was "safe." He wished Melissa could see this quality in Olivia. She could not see the God-given gifts Olivia had been blessed with. Jack knew Olivia was headed for great things one day, and wished Melissa could see it too.

"Thanks," Jack said hastily, grabbing his sunflower seeds, and walking out. The bell on the door rang slightly as he pushed it open.

Stepping off the porch, he heard a voice behind him. "That's a nice young lady you got there," said the old man.

"Yeah, she keeps me entertained," Jack said without even breaking stride, "she's one of a kind."

"She told me where you are headed."

This brought Jack to a stop. He turned around, "Oh yeah?"

"Sir, I only got one piece of advice for ya."

"And what's that?"

"Turn around…go back to where you came from!"

This caught Jack off guard. Looking down and shaking his head with a slight smile, he mustered the only response he could under his breath, "I wish I could."

☊

Their destination was Singleton, Illinois, Melissa's hometown. Melissa had insisted they move closer to her father; she felt that he could help with Olivia, possibly taking some of the strain off their marriage.

Both Jack and Melissa worked outside the home. Jack had worked for a local software company just outside the Denver area as an IT manager. He loved his job and his coworkers and they all got along great. It was very hard to give up his job, but he was willing to do anything to save his marriage. Melissa gave up a part-time job working at a small floral shop near where they lived on the south side of Denver. Melissa didn't have to work, Jack made plenty of money, but she always insisted she needed to get out of the house. Jack didn't know much about her work, but he always tried to be supportive and encourage her in it.

Jack felt there was something else odd about this move. Melissa wasn't planning on going back to work once in Singleton. This didn't make sense to him, if she was feeling stressed in Denver why didn't she just quit her job instead of insisting that they move? He tried to talk this through with Melissa, but he felt she was past the point of listening to reason and logic. Moving to Illinois, although it was a long ways away, was worth it to Jack if much of the stress would subside.

Singleton was a small, quiet community with a population of about two thousand. It was situated quietly off of Highway 34, thirty-five miles from Interstate 74 in Western Illinois. Everyone seemed to know everyone, along with their family history. It was a tight knit community. People who grew up in Singleton didn't leave, Melissa being a rare exception. There was also a patriotic feeling about the town. The citizens loved it. They felt they were part of one of the greatest American small towns in history, and their families were the reason for it.

There wasn't much crime in Singleton, in fact, there wasn't any! It was a squeaky–clean town. A couple of years ago it was big news that an elderly woman had taken a baseball bat and smashed a couple of windows in her house in an angry rage. Kind of odd, but that was the extent of the crime in town. It sort of seemed like the people lived in fear of messing up their town's reputation, which was basically unheard of. People outside of town knew little or nothing about it. The town was basically out of the way. It wasn't a town someone would drive through to get to Chicago, Peoria, or anywhere. It was a totally secluded community. Jack had not even seen a delivery truck so much as pass through, let alone stop. The citizens and business owners usually drove to Moline or Peoria for supplies.

Even though Singleton was a small community, it seemed to be quite prosperous. There were many farmers who seemed to be doing well, despite the tough economic situations facing farmers. There also a few private businesses: a café, a floral shop, a small gym, small grocer, and others. The biggest business in town was a small software designer where Jack had applied and found a job. His day-to-day would be a lot more routine and nowhere near as exciting as his position in Denver, but it all seemed to be a small sacrifice if it meant saving his marriage.

Though the businesses in Singleton were doing quite well, the main source of affluence was not centered on the businesses, but rather a person, Melissa's father, Alexander David Wellington VI, or Alex. He was the talk of the town. He practically owned half of it. People and businesses rented from him, and the businesses he didn't rent to, he owned. He didn't hold any political office, but he had the real power. He advised the city on large purchases and city planning. The mayor and city council seemed powerless compared to the power he wielded. People seemed to love, fear, and admire him. He was the reason Singleton was what it was today. Though the people didn't appear to leave the town much, Alex traveled quite a bit, mainly to Chicago, but he was also known to travel far and wide, including overseas.

Melissa's mother had died unexpectedly a few years ago. Melissa never talked much about her. It was a suicide. Jack didn't know many of the details. He could tell it was a sore subject, not just for the family, but also for the town. It was one of those things the people frowned upon, fearing that the town's reputation was somehow in jeopardy. Jack always wanted to ask more questions concerning Melissa's mother, Claudia, but Melissa would always respond to his questions in either anger or silence.

Jack had never been fond of Singleton. In fact, he hated it! The people's love for their town frankly got on his nerves. It almost felt like the people loved their town more than they did their own families. Jack was looked at as an outsider by the town folk. This was probably because he did not share the same sentiment for it. He had only come to visit a couple of times with Melissa, and hadn't been back since Olivia's adoption. In previous visits Jack always felt strange being there. While in town by himself the people would stare at him, and would not carry a conversation with him. Melissa would take time to introduce him to her acquaintances, and this was the only time the people would talk to him.

Socially, Jack expected things to be much worse upon arriving in Singleton. Everyone probably knew about their marriage problems and would most likely side with Melissa. To make matters worse, the cell phone tower near Singleton had recently been destroyed in a violent storm. For the time being there was absolutely no cell phone reception with any carrier. Thinking about this gave Jack a greater feeling of isolation. It would be much harder to make a private call back home. Through it all Jack was determined to make this experience in Singleton different. He would work as hard as he could to make this new life work for him, for Melissa, and for Olivia.

"Almost there," Jack said. They currently traveling in the hour long stretch from the Quad Cities to Singleton. The trip from Denver to Singleton was not in itself exciting, but this part seemed exceptionally long. The

Mississippi River bore the last bit of scenery, and from here on it was just flat Illinois land.

Chapter 3

The Averys arrived at their new home at about ten o'clock in the morning. Jack wanted to stay overnight with his uncle in Dubuque rather than arriving at their new home so late at night. Olivia loved Jack's uncle Frank. She had begged her Dad to stop at his house on the way. Of course, Melissa was not very thrilled at the idea, but eventually gave in, knowing that this would eliminate a trip in the near future.

Their new home was a small ranch style house on about a third of an acre of land in a quiet suburban neighborhood. It was a very faint blue with dark blue shutters. It was in good shape. They had never actually seen the house in person. Melissa's father purchased the house for them. Jack didn't like the idea of renting a home without seeing it, neither was he thrilled about the idea of having

Alex as his new landlord, but in the end he gave in knowing that Alex was wise enough to find them a nice place. The plan was for the Averys to rent for six months to a year until they became established in Singleton, and then potentially buy a home.

"Welcome to our new home!" Jack said pulling into the driveway.

"Yay, I love it, Daddy," said Olivia. She had always seen the move as a new adventure in life, but the house wasn't the reason she was excited. She really wanted the chance to explore her new town. She saw some of the wooded hills on their way in, and that was the main reason for her excitement. Who knows what she would find in those woods?

"Well, why don't we unpack a few things, and then head off for an early lunch," Jack suggested.

"Great idea, Daddy, can I pick out my room first?" Olivia asked while climbing out of the car, and running up the front steps.

Melissa was not thrilled with Olivia's excitement, "Jack, you have to remember to keep her calm. Singleton is not like Denver. This town doesn't take well to kids behaving like Olivia. In this town the kids are orderly, behaved, and…"

"Melissa, please calm down, Olivia is just enjoying these moments and the new home. She's probably excited to meet some new friends as well; just…please let her be."

"Jack, you don't understand Singleton, and I'm beginning to think you never will."

Jack didn't respond to this comment. He didn't care to understand Singleton. He wasn't going to let this town control or pressure him like it did the other citizens, nor was he going to let it oppress Olivia's attitude.

Getting out of the station wagon, Jack headed to the back of the trailer they pulled from Denver. They had sold most of their furniture upon leaving. Alex said he would help furnish some of the basic necessities. He opened the back of the packed trailer and grabbed a couple of duffle bags. Olivia was swinging on a new porch swing, obviously installed by Alex.

"Honey, not too hard," Jack instructed. Olivia jumped with the swing still in motion. She was anxious to see her new home.

Melissa, walking up the steps, fished in her purse for the key her father sent. Melissa found the key and opened the door. Jack was stunned by what he saw.

Alex had not just furnished the house, but furnished it in a magnificent fashion. Their living room area was beautiful. There were two nice leather couches seated in an L-shape, both in view of a large flat screen TV, mounted perfectly on the wall. The floors were a dark mahogany wood with a few rugs placed in high-traffic areas. Alex had a dining room table brought in, along with chairs. The kitchen was also fully furnished: utensils, pots, pans, spices, etc. There were basic necessities in the refrigerator to last them a few days. They walked around admiring their new home. It was a serious upgrade from their place in Denver.

"I love it, Daddy, can I go pick out my..." Olivia was interrupted by a knock on the open door.

"How do you like it?" said the all too familiar voice.

All three turned at once to see Melissa's father standing at the door. He was dressed in a three piece suit like he had just returned from some sort of business affair. He kept his grey hair much too long for a man of his age. Jack thought it gave him an evil look. He was roughly six feet, three inches tall, and skinny. He had begun to walk with a slight limp in his old age, which restricted him to a cane. He stood expressionless at the doorway.

"Father!" Melissa shouted, walking over to give him a hug. Jack had always been jealous of Melissa and her father's relationship. He always felt, or better yet, *knew* they were hiding something from him. He wondered if one day he would wake up to find that this was all just a sham. At his worst point he wondered if Alex was even Melissa's true father.

"And how's my little granddaughter?" Alex asked, bending over slightly to receive a hug. Olivia had never been very fond of her grandpa. He was never a part of her life. He never called on her birthday, and she'd only seen him once when he came to visit. During that visit, she didn't like the way her grandfather ordered her father around and was generally disrespectful of him.

Without saying a word, Olivia walked over and gave Alex a half-hearted hug.

"There, that wasn't so bad, was it?" Alex said with a small chuckle in his voice. Alex had a raspy voice that sounded like it was about to wear out at any moment.

"Thanks for doing this for us, it's... nice," Jack commented while reaching to shake Alex's hand.

Alex, also extending his hand, replied, "You're welcome, anything to help with this process. You should find everything you need around the house, except your phone. The phone company had to put in new lines, so they won't be in for a few days."

Everyone could see that Jack was not thrilled with this situation. He, of course, didn't like the idea of moving here and he thought of Alex's generous gifts as just a way for him to seize more control of their lives. And now without his land line working he would feel completely cut off from his family back home in Denver. This was not what he wanted to hear.

"Well, listen, we are just going to get settled and then maybe go grab a bite to eat before...." Jack wasn't able to finish.

"Well, there's no need, I'll have my men here unload your car and trailer. I'm also going to have them do a little patch work on certain areas of the roof. In the mean-time, I know a great place in Kewanee where we can grab some lunch. I'd love to take you there." Alex had hired a couple of workmen who were waiting in the driveway.

Jack was not keen on any of this. They had just been on the road for the last two and a half days, and a long drive to Kewanee was not what Jack wanted at all. He was looking forward to unpacking with Olivia, and getting some take out from one of the local cafes. He had planned for them to have a nice picnic in one of the local parks.

"Listen, we really appreciate it, but I think we're looking forward to a little down time being out of the car," Jack reasoned.

"Jack, don't talk to my father like that!" Melissa spat back, "he's done so much for us, the least you could do is give him a little respect."

Jack couldn't believe she was talking to him like this. "I know, Dear, but think about Olivia," he pulled Melissa aside, lowering his voice, "she's been cooped up in a car for two days, and you know she's anxious to get settled and relax." Olivia, at this time, was checking out the rest of the house.

"My father has been nothing but nice to you and this is how you repay him, Jack Avery! Listen, if we're going to make this new life work you are going to have to think about someone other than yourself."

"Listen, Melissa, all I'm saying is that we should take some time to do something as a family, to just relax. Olivia needs it."

"Don't you dare try to blame this on Olivia. This is about you!"

"Melissa, come on," Jack said trying to reason with her, even though he knew she was not going to be persuaded.

"Jack, we are starting this new life out right. If my father wants to take us to dinner, then we are going to let him."

Jack knew there was no chance in trying to be rational anymore. He knew this battle was not worth fighting.

♋

The drive home from Kewanee in Alex's large SUV was quiet, save for a little classical music playing on the radio. They had stayed at the restaurant late into the afternoon. It was a very upscale restaurant for a small town. Alex and the owner seemed to be business associates; Alex knew many people at the restaurant which slowed the progress of the meal. All of this annoyed Jack. He had great plans to unpack together as a family before taking a break and going to a park with Olivia. He did not like how this day was going.

Alex and Melissa were seated up front with Jack and Olivia in the second row. Jack could see Alex periodically looking at him in the rear view mirror. He tried not to look, but felt Alex was trying to study his body language.

"So, are you excited about the new job, Jack?" Alex broke the silence.

"Sort of, to tell you the truth, I'm kind of just looking forward to taking the rest of today and tomorrow to relax. The road took its toll on me."

"I understand. Well from what I understand the fellows are looking forward to having you on the team," Alex said reassuringly. Jack thought this was laughable. The folks of Singleton never took well to outsiders and he couldn't imagine anyone excited about him being in town.

"Thanks!" Jack responded.

Singleton Software was a small software company. It was not very well known but it had its own niche customers. Jack would be working in a cubicle on the first floor. This didn't excite him at all; he loved to be on his feet, meeting with people. The only upside was that he would be isolated and not having to interact with the people of Singleton. Most of the people he had met from the town gave him the creeps.

♋

They arrived home a few minutes before four in the afternoon, a lot later than Jack had anticipated. It was raining heavily.

Upon arriving, Jack noticed that Alex's movers had unloaded the trailer, and had unpacked their boxes for them. Even though their trailer and station wagon were packed full of boxes, compared to other couples their age, Jack and Melissa had not accumulated many belongings. Even when they were dating Jack was surprised at how few possessions Melissa had in her Denver apartment.

The men seemed to have unpacked everything but the Avery's personal suitcases. Even small details like their welcome mat were placed outside their front door. Jack was thankful they had detached the trailer from their station wagon and apparently returned it to the nearest U-Haul dealer about twenty-five miles outside of town.

As they entered the house, Jack could tell that Olivia was obviously disappointed. She had wanted to spend time arranging her new room. Melissa threw her purse on the kitchen counter, walked into their master bedroom and shut the door. She was obviously upset about the argument they had earlier. Jack knew it wasn't a good a time to run after her and maybe he should just let her cool down. Besides, he felt Olivia needed more of his attention at this point.

"Hey, Sweetie," he said calling out to Olivia, "why don't we break this house in with a good game of Risk!"

"Daddy, I don't think we should do that."

"Why's that, Honey?"

"I would hate to see you cry after I take over the world."

"Is that so?" Jack said with a chuckle in his voice.

Jack and Olivia played late into the evening. It was about ten thirty before they finally called it quits for the night. They had never really played a whole Risk game in one sitting; it would take hours. They usually broke it up over a three or four day period. Jack never went easy on Olivia. She was a good sport and had a tough demeanor. She wouldn't have liked it if she thought her father was not playing his best. Olivia first learned to play only a few weeks after she was adopted. She had seen her father play with his brother, Steve. She was fascinated right away and latched onto the game.

"Well, I think I'm about ready to hit the hay, Darling," Jack said, stretching and yawning.

"I think it's about time for me too, Daddy," Olivia agreed.

"It's been a long couple of days, I could really use an early bedtime."

They hadn't seen Melissa all evening. She had stayed in the bedroom since the trip to Kewanee. Jack had checked on her a few times. She was watching the news on a TV her father had set up. She said she didn't want to be disturbed.

They were cleaning up some plates and cups they had used for snacks when Olivia spoke up, "Daddy!"

"Yes, Dear?"

"Do you think Mom will get better now that we are here?"

Jack didn't know how to respond. He didn't like talking about their marriage problems with Olivia, but things had gotten so bad he couldn't hide everything from Olivia. It was becoming obvious to everyone that their marriage was not going well. Jack stopped what he was doing and placed both hands on the table. With a slight sigh Jack responded quietly, "I hope so, Olivia, I really do."

"I just hate it, Daddy," Olivia said with both anger and sorrow in her voice, "I hate how she treats you. I hate how she ignores me. I hate..."

"Shhh, it's all right, Olivia," Jack bent down on one knee, giving Olivia a hug as he tried to comfort her. "We're going to work on this, Sweetie, everyday."

Jack let go and looked straight into Olivia's eyes, "Know this, Dear, I'm going to do whatever it takes for us. I'll climb any mountain, make any sacrifice to make you happy. We are going to do this."

"I know, Daddy, I love you," Olivia said giving him a tight squeeze.

"I love you too," Jack said returning the hug, "Let's get some rest, Dear."

Olivia hadn't spent much time in her room. She was a little bummed she didn't get to pick out her own room, but her grandfather did choose the bigger and best of the two spare bedrooms, and the movers had done a great job of setting it up. It looked beautiful. The only thing left to be unpacked was her large duffle bag full mostly of clothes and personal items. The movers had set it on her bed. Upon entering her room, she opened it up to grab her toiletries. Looking around her bag she noticed things looked a little out of place, like someone had been fishing around in her bag.

Jack snuck into his bedroom. Melissa appeared to already be asleep. He was amazed that even in a new location their marriage picked up right where they left off. He thought Melissa would have taken time this evening to spend with the family. He was also surprised that Melissa didn't bother to make dinner. She enjoyed cooking and Jack thought she would be anxious to try out her new kitchen or at the very least join Olivia and him for sandwiches and chips. She just stayed in the bedroom and watched TV all evening.

Jack grabbed his toothbrush from his bag and headed into the master bathroom. He was very careful not to wake Melissa. Jack turned on the light in the bathroom, and took a look around. He hadn't had much opportunity to check out their bathroom. It was nice. Walking over to the sink, he turned the water on and bent over to wash his face. He splashed a little water on his face, stood back up looking straight into the mirror. He picked up a towel to wipe the water off his face when he heard a knock on the bedroom door.

Jack turned the bathroom light off and headed toward the bedroom door. He opened it up to find Olivia standing in the hallway looking puzzled.

"Hey, what is it?" he said curiously.

"Those men, those movers, Daddy, they took it, they stole it!"

Chapter 4

"Daddy, I know they stole it. It had to be them," Olivia protested.

"Honey, I'm sorry that it's missing, but I just don't think anyone would have a reason to steal it. I know it means a lot to you, but I don't think anyone else would want it," Jack said trying to calm her. "Listen, Olivia, I imagine it will turn up somewhere, maybe the movers found it and put it in an unusual spot."

"No, Daddy, I put it right in my duffle bag. I know I did. I packed it myself. I knew right where it was!"

"Listen, Sweetie, I know that box is very special to you, but I don't see any reason why someone would want to steal it."

"Daddy, I know those movers took it, and I think they took it for Grandpa."

"Olivia, don't be silly. I know Grandpa may come across a little…strange at times," Jack said as he tried to grasp for words, "but to steal your box? He would have no reason to, and besides he wouldn't know where to find it!"

"Daddy, listen to me!" Olivia pleaded.

None of Jack's reasoning resonated with Olivia. She would not hear any talk of the box being misplaced. In her mind she knew someone took it, and she believed Alex was behind it. She had never trusted her grandpa. She always felt that he never really loved her.

Jack, knowing that this was not a discussion he could win at the moment, decided to retreat, "All right, well, how about this, we get a good night's rest, and then in the morning we will look for it, and I will ask Grandpa if the movers saw or found anything."

"Ok, fine," Olivia said realizing that there wasn't anything else that could be done to locate the box that night.

"I love you, Sweetie."

"I love you too, Daddy."

"And don't worry about it, we will find it," Jack said trying to reassure Olivia.

Olivia walked back down the hallway to her room, feeling a little dejected. Jack watched as she entered her room and shut the door. He thought, "How could this only be our first day in Singleton?" It seemed as if so much drama had taken place already. Melissa was already upset with him, and Olivia claims that her Grandpa stole her box of items from her children's home.

When Olivia left St. Thomas Children's Home, along with a few sets of clothes, she brought a shoebox full of odd things she had collected over time: a child's bracelet, some rosary beads, a few dollars in change, candy, a small doll, and a few other loose items. Nothing Jack thought anyone else would want. It was mostly things that only Olivia would find special. The box itself was a women's old high heel shoebox. It was made a little sturdier than the average shoebox. It was a cream color, but had some discoloration from stains along with simple wear and tear on the exterior. Jack and Melissa never thought too much of the box. Melissa would sometimes make a passing comment on how Olivia ought to get rid of it. Possibly Melissa thought it would help Olivia forget about her past life and adjust to her new family.

Jack headed back to the bathroom and continued where he left off washing his face and brushing his teeth. He couldn't get the thought out of his head, *Did Alex steal the shoebox?* The whole notion seemed absurd. What would he want with her box? It was a crazy idea, but somehow Jack thought it was possible. Maybe this was some sort of scheme by Melissa to get rid of it. She had some very odd quirks lately, and possibly something about Olivia's old box set her off. It seemed strange, but the more Jack thought about it, the more it seemed possible to him, and the more it angered him. What if Melissa orchestrated a plan in order to take Olivia's box?

In midst of brushing his teeth, he stopped, put his toothbrush down and stared deeply at his reflection in the mirror. *I'm not going to be able to sleep with these ideas going through my mind.* He thought, *What would Melissa say about Olivia's idea of the movers taking her box?* He thought he ought to ask Melissa point blank about it. Maybe it wasn't stolen, maybe Melissa put it in a different spot, or had it thrown away. Either way Jack felt he had to ask her.

He finished getting himself ready, turned out the lights, and climbed into bed. Melissa stirred slightly in the covers. He couldn't sleep until he got this somewhat resolved. Sitting up, he shook Melissa, "Melissa, Melissa," he said in a whisper.

Melissa turned over to face Jack, slightly opening her eyes, "What is it, Jack?"

"Olivia can't find her box, and I was wondering if you'd seen it."

"Can't this wait till morning?"

"She thinks one of the movers took it while we were out to lunch with your father."

"Jack, that's crazy, can we talk about this in the morning?" Melissa said, getting angrier by the second.

"I don't know, I just remember you asking her a few times to get rid of it, and I didn't know if maybe over the course of the trip or the move, you might have..." Jack wasn't able to finish.

Melissa turned over, seemingly wide awake for the moment, "Jack, how dare you suggest such a thing? I'm trying to make this life work here in Singleton, and for you to think that I would do such a thing is totally absurd. I've done so much for this family and..."

"Whoa, calm down, Dear," Jack said putting his hands up, "I was just asking if maybe you saw it on the trip or..."

"Jack Avery, shut up! I can't believe how you've been acting since we arrived. First you act rudely around my father, and now this!"

"Melissa, calm down, let me explain!"

"You know what . . . GET OUT!"

"What?" Jack was dumbfounded. All he wanted was to explain himself and what he was thinking. Melissa had blown up before but never like this.

"Just get out for now! I do not want to see your face tonight!" Melissa shouted.

"Fine," Jack said, picking up his pillow to sleep on the couch. Jack knew there was nothing else he could have said. He thought maybe he should not have brought this up in the first place. It was most likely his distrust in Alex that got him thinking. He thought, *Why did I not at least wait until morning to bring this up?* He was kicking himself as he headed for the living room couch.

He could not believe how this day had turned out. He thought this had to be one of the longest days of his life, and it was just the beginning of life in Singleton.

He lay on the couch for a while before realizing that he couldn't sleep. He grabbed the remote. He was so stirred from his confrontation with Melissa that he felt a little Letterman would help him sleep. He was willing to try anything to get his mind off the day. Alex had set them up with a nice cable package. All of these amenities left Jack in a quandary. He loved all the nice things, but knowing that they came from Alex just made him sick. After watching Letterman Jack flipped through the channels. He turned the TV off around midnight.

The couch was very comfortable. It was a nice new black leather couch. His body sank down in it when he sat or laid on it. Jack actually thought it was more comfortable than their bed. Another benefit was that he didn't have to worry about bumping into Melissa in the night. She had always been a light sleeper, and never wanted to be so much as touched during the night. As bad as the day had been, at least it was over and he was going to get a good night's rest.

♋

As he lay on the couch Jack thought back to their first big fight about two years ago. Throughout their dating relationship and early on in their marriage, Jack had always submitted to Melissa's demands and allowed her to control him. He was mesmerized by her beauty and charm, and was truly blinded by his love for her. He did not want anything to mess up their relationship. Jack changed after they adopted Olivia. He loved his little girl and realized he needed to be the father she never had. He knew he had to step up and take more of a leadership role in their family.

Just like their fight from earlier in the day, their first big fight also revolved around Melissa's father. He had stopped to visit the family while passing through Denver on business. They were eating together and Olivia was jabbering away about their last camping trip.

"I didn't think I could stay three nights out in the woods. I thought I might want to come home, but it was fun.

I got cold one night, but then Daddy built this huge fire and . . ."

Melissa interrupted, "Olivia, I think you should give it a little rest. Grandpa had a busy day, and besides, you need to finish your carrots."

"Ok, well, let me just tell him about the fish we caught in the lake. They were huge and Daddy about slipped in . . ."

"Olivia, I said that's enough!"

"Maybe later, Child," Alex added in his quiet raspy voice. Olivia looked heartbroken.

Jack piped in, "So, Alex, how is business these days, how are things going in Singleton?"

"It is well. You know, a small town; not much happens. It's not like here in Denver."

Jack loved his city, "Yeah, good ole' Denver, always something going on here, but it's also a good location to make an easy escape to see some backcountry."

Alex looked a little puzzled, "But all the crime, Jack. You must think about your family. It's probably not safe here at times."

"It comes with any big city. But it's like my father always said, 'Don't go looking for trouble and trouble won't find you.'"

"Well Jack, if you'd ever consider it, I could find you a nice spot in Singleton, probably get you a position at our software company. It would be a good life," Alex said with a wave of his hand.

Jack chuckled a little, "Thanks, but no thanks. This is the place for us. There is nowhere else I'd rather be. We love it here."

"Jack!" Melissa interjected, "you shouldn't blow my father off like that. That should be something we should at least think about. Singleton is a very prestigious town, and landing a job there is no easy feat."

This caught Jack completely off guard. "Well, I do appreciate the generosity, Alex, but we're doing just fine here in Denver."

"But, Jack, don't you think we should at least consider what my father is offering?"

"No!" Jack said with an air of finality. He was getting a little angry at Melissa for springing this on him so abruptly.

"Could you excuse us, please?" Melissa said standing up and throwing her napkin down on the table. Jack got up to follow her to their bedroom. It was there that he first saw her temper.

"Jack Avery, we need to listen to my father. This might be an opportunity for us. You know the power and influence he has. He might be able to help us. You could land a real job, possibly even making six figures. I want us to at least think about this."

"Melissa, what is there to think about? We love it here," Jack could tell Melissa was getting angrier as he spoke, "Olivia has her friends, and my family is here. I feel like we are just now getting settled. We can't pick up and leave now, nor do I want to!"

"Listen to yourself," Melissa pleaded, "This is a chance for you get away from that crummy job of yours. You could double or triple our income. This is something I want to do someday and I would like you to at least consider it, and besides, maybe it could help us tame Olivia a little."

"What are you talking about?" Jack interjected.

"You know what I'm talking about. Olivia just has too much energy sometimes. A quiet place like Singleton might be what we need to help calm her down. It would be good for her," Melissa said putting her hand on Jack's arm.

He quickly pulled his arm away. "Olivia is fine the way she is. She doesn't need to calm down. I appreciate her energy, her spunk. I feel like this is just a way for your father to control us."

"Jack, don't you bring him into this. This is about you!"

"Come on, Melissa, you're letting him influence you. We don't want to move to Singleton!"

Melissa was furious, and the conversation had gotten out of hand, "You're pathetic, you know?"

Jack couldn't believe his ears, "Where did that come from? This has nothing to do with your father. I do not want to move to Singleton!"

"This conversation is over Jack," Melissa said, walking out of their bedroom, slamming the door behind her.

Jack slumped down onto the bed, exhausted and confused with what had just happened.

Now lying on his couch in Singleton, he realized the irony behind their first real fight. *I guess at the end of the day*

Melissa won that one, he thought to himself. These were memories he longed to forget and put behind him. He was tired and ready to get some sleep. Tomorrow could be another rough day.

♋

"BANG!"

He heard a loud crash coming from the outside. He was not sure how long he had been asleep. He heard another one, "BANG!" What was going on? This wasn't the sound of a gun firing, but rather something hitting his house. What on earth could this be?

He got up and took a quick look through the blinds out of his front window. He couldn't see much. Singleton was always known for being a tranquil city and he wondered what hit his house.

He grabbed his Louisville Slugger bat that had been placed in a closet with some winter coats. He didn't own a gun, but he thought this was the next best thing for protection. He would do whatever it took to defend his family.

He waited beside the front door for about five minutes before he decided to open it. He unlocked the door and peeked out. The night air felt cool. He could see just a little with the street lights shining from the road. He noticed nothing out of the ordinary at first glance. He thought the threat, or whatever it was, was probably gone by now.

He opened the door a little more and stuck his head out, looking around...nothing! It seemed safe enough to have a closer look. He opened the door fully and stepped out onto his porch. The driveway and yard were empty, nothing looked vandalized. The road was even quiet and he couldn't hear any cars in the distance.

Jack turned to inspect the front of his house. It was then that Jack saw what had been done to it. He couldn't believe it!

Chapter 5

"Eggs?" Jack whispered under his breath.

The yolk was still running down the front of their house. The shells were there, sitting broken on their porch. This whole situation was confusing for a few reasons. Why would anyone want to egg their house? They hadn't even been in Singleton a full day. There was no time to make enemies. Jack considered that it could be an enemy of Alex's that did not want to face him. Or maybe an old boyfriend of Melissa's that was just waiting for a way to vent his frustrations. None of these ideas made sense to Jack. Petty crimes like this weren't supposed to happen in Singleton.

Just my luck! Jack thought, watching the yolk drip from the front of his house. On second thought, throwing eggs at a house didn't seem like a way to get even in a vendetta against his wife or father-in-law. It was probably just some kid looking for cheap thrills, hopefully nothing more.

He thought he might as well clean it up now. Even though it was late, his adrenaline was going strong and he wouldn't sleep at this point. He remembered when they drove up to the house early that morning that an old hose had been left from the previous owners. Hopefully just a good spray would get the egg off the siding and then he could deal with the rest of this situation in the morning.

Jack stepped off the porch with his bare feet. His pajama pants blew slightly in the wind. His yard looked well kept, so he had no fear of stepping on anything unwanted. He walked over to the left side of the house where he had first seen the hose. It was lying in a pile and looked quite tangled. Fiddling around with it, he stretched it out toward the road. Some of the tangles came out as he stretched it farther and farther.

He was surprised when his heel touched the edge of the sidewalk. It was cold. He pulled the hose further, stepping both feet onto the sidewalk. A tangle caught, ripping the hose nozzle out of his hand and onto the sidewalk. Reaching down to pick it up, he noticed something to his left...or rather someone.

A teenage boy was watching him from about fifty yards away at the corner of the block. He was dressed in jeans and was wearing a black pull-over jacket with the hood covering his head. Jack stood up, wondering what he was doing. *Could this be the kid who egged my house*? Jack thought, *Or maybe this kid saw something.*

He wanted to yell out at him, but being the middle of the night he didn't want to risk waking the neighbors. He took a few steps toward the boy, who looked to be maybe seventeen and about six feet in height. From Jack's perspective, he didn't look suspicious, just curious. Jack walked closer to the boy. When he got within twenty-five yards of him, the boy took off running down an intersecting street. He was gone. Jack thought about running after him, but decided otherwise. It was the middle of the night and it had been a long day. He was barefoot and also confused about the whole matter. All of this was very strange. He never could have predicted the way this day would go.

Jack retreated back to his house, pulling the hose with him. He walked up onto his porch and began washing the front window. Everything was soaked. He figured the egg was so diluted that it would not cause much harm. Given the very small slant of the porch, he figured all the water would run off over time. Overall, Jack didn't care, it was late.

Who was that boy? Jack thought he could identify the boy if he saw him around the neighborhood. He thought about calling the police in the morning, but at the time it seemed like a big hassle. The town of Singleton might freak out over this incident. They weren't used to crime, so any new gossip, no matter how small, was big news. Jack thought that if the boy was found out, the locals might crucify him. The people of Singleton probably wouldn't deal lightly with crime, so this kid would probably face a large misdemeanor and community service, as well as family shame. Jack thought he'd rather not put a kid through all that.

Jack rolled the hose back to the side of the house where he found it, and turned the water off. Possibly this time he could get some sleep. He entered the house as quickly as he could. He sat down on the couch, and began taking off his slippers.

"Daddy," he heard Olivia's soft voice coming from the hallway. She peeked out into the living room.

"Yes?"

"What were you doing outside?"

"Someone threw some eggs at our house. I wanted to hose it off before it dried," Jack said, not being the least bit shy about the matter. He was usually very honest with Olivia. She could tell he was a little angry.

"Why'd they do that?"

"I don't know, Olivia," Jack said with a little bit of frustration in his voice, "It was probably just some stupid kid thinking it would be fun to egg the new people's house."

"Well, that's awfully rude!" Olivia said with a pre-teen attitude in her voice.

"Goodnight, Olivia!" Jack said with finality in his voice. He was ready to end the conversation and get to bed.

"Goodnight, Daddy, I love you."

"I love you too."

Olivia didn't ask about Jack sleeping on the couch. It had become a normal thing for her mother and father to be at odds. She did not like it, but she dealt with it. In her mind, she was just happy to have a family of her own. She would always say she loved the nuns who took care of her, but as all the other children in home would say, the dream is always to be adopted by a family. And though her family was not perfect, it was indeed a family.

Jack couldn't sleep. He was caught thinking about the events of the day. How was he going to make his marriage work? Melissa seemed to be totally shut off to him. She would not listen to anything. At a breaking point a few months back in Denver she had thrown a wine glass at him. That seemed to be the point at which Jack knew they needed to get help. He seriously considered divorcing her at that point, but his pastor advised him otherwise. Jack fought this advice until finally he decided that fighting for his marriage was best for Olivia.

Jack had never been much of a spiritual man until Olivia was adopted. Growing up, he was used to going to church every Sunday, but through his college and adult life he had gotten out of the habit. It was actually Olivia who convinced him to start attending regularly. Olivia learned the Bible fervently under the nuns at the children's home. They would take her to Mass and other special children events at a nearby cathedral. Jack's parents considered themselves Baptist, and for the last three years he took Olivia to the 3rd St. Baptist Church in Denver, where his parents attended. His brother Steve was recently added to the church as an Associate Pastor. Though the Averys were not heavily involved, Jack and Olivia were there most Sundays.

Melissa never cared much for church and Jack never pressed her about it. When they were dating they had a few surface conversations about God and church, but nothing very substantial. Jack was always so blinded by her beauty that he never wanted to upset her or talk about any issues that he thought might cause friction in their relationship. At times his parents gave him subtle warnings about how he was being controlled by her. Even though in the back of his mind he knew they were right, he didn't want to hear it. He loved Melissa and was captivated by her.

Jack thought long and hard while looking up at the ceiling. How would he make things work with Alex? He didn't like the idea of his father-in-law having so much power over the direction of his family. Should he just submit to some of his demands and wishes, and hope that his marriage would work out? How would he mend the relationship between Olivia and Alex? She didn't like her grandfather one bit. This was not going to sit well with Melissa. She adored her father, and she was not going to put up with Olivia not showing her father the respect she thought he deserved.

He wanted to scream! *Why did I move here*, he thought. There seemed to be so many problems with this "new life" in Singleton. How was he ever going to work through these situations? "God help me!" he prayed. Jack was not a praying man, but he knew when he needed help. "I can't do this on my own. Help me God! Everything seems so hard. I don't know what to do!" Jack whispered his prayer under his breath. He always felt like he didn't know how to pray.

♋

Jack's mind drifted back to a conversation he had with his brother six years back. They were fishing off a dock near Steve's home. It was getting late into the evening. Jack's wedding was a couple of weeks away and his brother Steve was begging him for one more late night fishing excursion before the big day. They were sitting on the edge of the dock with their poles in the water, hoping for a bite at any moment. It was a beautiful evening, with the crickets in full song.

Jack was carrying on about the Broncos, "I can't believe they lost another one. At this rate I don't think we are going to make the playoffs. San Diego is catching us and has been playing great. In my opinion I think the coach has got to go."

"Yeah, it makes me long for the days of Elway," Steve added, tugging his pole a little, trying to see if there was any tension in the line.

"Well, hopefully they can hold on. One of my coworkers said he possibly could swing Melissa and me tickets if there is a playoff run."

"Does she keep up with the games?"

Jack chuckled a little, "Oh yeah, we watch them all together."

"It must be great having a fiancée who is as big of a Broncos fan as you are," Steve added.

Jack didn't know how to take this comment from Steve. At times Jack thought his brother might be a little jealous of his relationship with Melissa. Steve was single, but really wanted a girl of his own. Jack tried to give him a little encouragement, "Listen man, your time will come. Just be patient. Keep your head up!"

Steve was caught off guard, "Oh, no, I didn't mean it like that. I just remember you always said you wanted to find a girl who was a real Broncos fan, and I guess your wish finally came true."

"It's great man! I love her! I can't wait for this wedding. I am one lucky man."

Steve stared off into the distance. He looked to be in deep in thought, like something was bothering him. Jack could see he had something on his mind, "What are you thinking, Bro? Is everything ok?"

Steve took a deep breath and looked straight at his brother, "Are you sure you want to go through with it?"

"What are you talking about?" Jack was shocked, "Of course I want to go through with it. I've never landed a girl like Melissa before. She's awesome. I'm lucky to have her."

"Listen, Jack, I don't know man, but something tells me she is not right for you. In some ways I still feel like we just don't know much about her."

"Come on Steve! Don't be crazy, man, she's perfect. I don't know what you're thinking."

"Jack, the way she talks to you and orders you around at times is a little concerning. I feel like you're following her around like a little puppy." Jack and Steve had always been very close and they were not afraid to speak very open and honestly with each other.

"Steve, you've seen Melissa! Before she met me, I bet she had a hundred guys lining up to get her number. She's a real catch! I want her to be mine, and I don't want to wait any longer."

Steve put his pole down. He wanted to be sure his brother knew he was serious, "Jack, don't you think you are rushing into things just a little? I mean you don't know much about her family or where she stands on matters of faith. You need to really think things through. I know that I'm speaking for both Dad and Mom too; we would really like to see you postpone for a few months. We think it would just be good for . . ."

Steve wasn't able to finish. Jack stood up and threw his fishing pole to the ground, "I can't believe you! Is this what this is about? You trying to talk me out of this wedding?"

Steve stood up. He now was on the defensive, "No, Jack! I just...want to see you make the right decision. I mean we all have some concerns about Melissa and don't think she is . . ."

Jack was getting very angry, "Ok, you know what, little bro, this conversation is over. I know what this is about! You are jealous. You are afraid to be some single thirty year old man while your brother is happy with a wonderful wife." He spoke, jamming his finger into his brother's chest, "Here's another thing, don't throw all this faith garbage at me either. You think just because you are trying to become some ministry boy that you are more spiritual than I am. You need to just cool off, Steve."

Jack began to walk away, off the dock. Steve yelled for him, "Come on, Bro! Don't be like that! I'm just looking out for you, man!"

"Well do me a favor and look somewhere else!" Jack said, walking away.

♋

That memory on the fishing dock haunted Jack for a while. It took a week before he and his brother spoke again. Jack had since apologized multiple times to Steve, and in hindsight Jack could see some of his brother's concerns. He was thankful to have a brother that was very forgiving. Over the past couple of years Jack spent many nights seeking counsel and advice from his younger brother.

It was past 1:30am when Jack was finally able to clear his head and fall asleep.

Chapter 6

Jack awoke to the sound of Olivia turning on the TV. Olivia, still in her pajamas, was eating a bowl of cereal with an overly large spoon on their new coffee table. Alex had thought to supply the Averys with a few sugared cereals for Olivia. At times he tried to win her love, but it still seemed so fake. Olivia turned on reruns from The Discovery Channel. Jack felt awful.

"Olivia, it's early," Jack moaned.

"Dad, can we go to the park today?"

"Maybe, but right now, I just want to sleep," Jack said pulling a blanket over his head.

Jack tried to fall back asleep, but his effort was in vain. The TV was too loud, and besides that, the bathroom was calling. Jack figured it was time to start the day.

Jack passed Melissa in the hallway on the way to the guest bathroom. She looked well-kempt, like she had already been up for an hour, getting ready for the day. "Good morning, Dear," Jack said, giving her a half smile.

"Good morning," she returned very matter-of-factly.

Entering the living room, Melissa was disappointed to find Olivia eating on their new coffee table. "Olivia, let's eat at the table please." Olivia, without questioning, got up from the coffee table and took her bowl to their kitchen table. She had learned not to challenge or question her mother. Melissa had never been open to discussing things with Olivia. She drew a hard line and never wanted it crossed.

Jack returned to the kitchen. He was hoping the night had given Melissa some time to cool off. He began making himself breakfast. "How'd everyone sleep last night?"

"Fine," Olivia answered, not even looking up from her cereal. She was not very talkative when she knew her mother was in a bad mood.

"How 'bout you, Honey?" Jack said, turning to Melissa.

"Ok," Melissa returned, "Jack, I want you to start working on the yard today. Certain areas are full of weeds, and the front bushes look awful."

"How 'bout I eat breakfast first."

"Jack, don't start!" Melissa countered.

"Melissa, I just want to relax, spend some time with you and Olivia today. Summer is almost over and I begin my job tomorrow. Let's just take some time to get started on the right foot." There was an obvious amount of frustration in

Jack's voice. Their family had gotten to the point where Jack and Melissa did not even try to hide their fights from Olivia.

Melissa shot back, "You don't understand! This is Singleton. People have high expectations for how a house looks. I'm not going to be known as the new wife in town with the terrible yard."

"Come on, Melissa, it was a tough day yesterday, and we just got in. I'm sure the people will understand."

"Jack, is that what this is about?" Melissa looked straight at him.

"What? I don't know what you are talking about."

"You are still upset about going with my father yesterday," Melissa said, nearly shouting.

"Listen, I just want to spend some time with you and Olivia," Jack pleaded. Olivia had left the room at this point. Over time she had grown tired of hearing her parents fight.

"Jack, you're hopeless!" Melissa said starting to walk away.

"Melissa, this has nothing to do with your father," Jack said, lying slightly. "After Olivia's box going missing and someone egging our house, I just thought . . ."

"What?" Melissa said turning back, walking closer.

"Yeah, Olivia can't find her box."

"No, I mean...our house was egged?" Melissa said inquisitively.

"Yeah, late last night as I was falling asleep."

This appeared to shock Melissa, "Who was it?"

"I don't know for sure. There were only a couple of eggs thrown. I cleaned them off the house. I never thought

63

something like this would happen here." Jack was quite upset about the situation, but he appreciated the fact that Melissa now seemed ready to listen.

"Did you see anyone?"

Jack thought for a second. Melissa loved her town, and she, like the rest of the people, would want to deal harshly with the perpetrator. If Jack suggested the boy he saw up the street, then he would probably be found and punished, whether innocent or guilty. The people of Singleton had set a precedent indicating that they would not put up with mischief. He concluded that Melissa did not need to know about him.

"No," Jack lied.

"I wonder if this is happening to others," Melissa said. Her tone had become quite softened at this point.

"I don't know. I'm just frustrated."

"Who would do such a thing?" Melissa wondered.

"Well, all I can say is that it wasn't a very nice house warming gift."

"We will have to keep our eyes open. Hopefully this won't happen again." Melissa said, looking straight at her husband. The tension between the two had relaxed. Jack was no longer upset about the eggs. The softened tone in Melissa's voice was worth it all. It seemed as if this was something with which she needed Jack's help. It was almost as if all of her anger toward Jack had been redirected toward the unknown criminal.

"Well, I don't know what we can do about it." Jack said, looking to change the subject. "So what are your plans for the day?"

"My father's coming over, and we are going to take a look at a few things around town."

"What kind of things?"

"Just a few shops, and maybe meet up with some people I used to know," Melissa said casually. This upset Jack just a little. It seemed like he ought to be accompanying Melissa with these tasks, not her father. But any irritation Jack felt about the situation was dispersed by the fact that Melissa was talking rationally with him. He really appreciated the tone of their conversation and was hoping it would last all morning.

"How about you?" Melissa returned the question.

"After breakfast I think Olivia and I will probably throw the baseball or check out that park I saw just outside our neighborhood and then...probably work on the yard."

♋

Alex slept in just a little that morning. In his older age he was getting used to going to bed early and waking up late. He had much to do today and he figured he best start the day.

He lived in a very large house. Not quite a mansion, but still the largest house in Singleton. It was located not far from the center of town. Everyone knew where it was located. It had been passed down through the family for years. It was a highly respected property, full of history.

He pulled off the covers and slipped on his slippers and robe. He was excited that Melissa was able to get her family to move back to Singleton. Things were working out just as he hoped. He loved getting his way. He couldn't help but smile as he washed his face. Jack was making things hard for Melissa, but Alex was thankful that Jack was caving into her demands.

After getting himself dressed and shaved, he was ready to go pick up his daughter. He had a full day planned. His slight limp made the steps in his home difficult to maneuver. A few years back he installed an elevator in his house. Many people in town did not approve of this dramatic renovation to his historic home, but were too frightened of Alex to speak up. It was such a landmark in their town that they did not want it to change.

He entered the elevator and pushed the button for the lower floor. He felt powerful every morning entering it. He knew that folks in town were upset about the renovation, but he didn't care. He liked the fact that he had the people of Singleton under his thumb. He could do whatever he wanted. The people lived in fear of him.

The elevator opened and he headed for the kitchen. He was a little stiff and would have to rely heavily on his cane today. Approaching the kitchen he saw things were out of place. What he found in the room utterly shocked him. There was glass on the floor. Someone had broken into his home.

He noticed the window above the sink was broken and completely knocked out. There was a little blood on the windowsill where the intruder had probably cut himself climbing in. This was the only window in the whole house not connected to his security system. Whoever broke in knew exactly what he was doing. This was not random but intentional.

Alex thought about calling the police but had second thoughts, knowing they were worthless. His methods and influence were a lot more effective than their crime scene investigations.

He was extremely angry. Nothing like this had ever happened. Could this have been someone in town? An outsider? He quickly looked around his home to see what had been taken or vandalized. This was not how he wanted to start the day. Someone would pay for this.

Chapter 7

The rest of the morning went smoothly for the Avery family. Since their earlier conversation about the egging, Melissa seemed very calm and understanding toward Jack and Olivia. She didn't even mind that Jack was waiting until the afternoon to work on the yard. He and Olivia had gotten a slow start on the day. Jack took his time showering and even managed to do a little unpacking before taking Olivia outside to throw the baseball. Olivia was enjoying herself, but Jack could tell that her mind was still on her missing shoebox. It was about noon.

"You all right?" he asked, catching a fly ball Olivia threw to him. She had a good arm for her age. She enjoyed playing baseball and softball but her favorite thing was just throwing with her father.

"Yeah."

"Are you still thinking about your box?"

"Yeah, I want to ask Grandpa if his men saw it," Olivia answered. It seemed that she had softened her initial accusation against her grandfather. Jack was encouraged by this.

"Well, he will be here before too long and you can ask him about it when he is here."

Occasionally some folks from the neighborhood would walk by. There was not much in the way of conversation with his neighbors. Most would just stare as they walked by. Everyone knew that they were the new family in town, and people in Singleton did not take too well to new folks. Jack tried to be friendly as people passed, but most were short with him, letting him know that he was not going to be welcomed in this town.

Jack thought the people may be looking down on Olivia and him for being outside throwing the baseball on a Sunday morning. Most people in Singleton regarded the day as sacred. There was only one church in town, and Jack made it clear that he was not going to attend the Singleton Newness Church. He hated everything about it, including the name. The service itself was very strange and like nothing he'd ever attended. Above that the people seemed bent on the idea that they had a special blessing from God that was above everyone else in the world. Of course Jack was not welcomed very warmly the one time he went. When it was settled that they were moving back to Singleton, Melissa did not even bother about asking him to go to church. She knew he wasn't going. Jack didn't care what his neighbors thought about him. It sort of made him proud to be disliked in a town he hated so much.

His mind was still on Olivia. He didn't want her to worry about the box. He was certain it would turn up somewhere. "How about this, why don't we stop now and get some lunch?

"Then can we go to the park, Daddy?"

"Sure, Sweetie."

Jack and Olivia raced from their front yard up to the front door, throwing their gloves in the corner of the porch. They figured they would be taking them later to the park, so there was no need to put them away.

♋

Jack and Olivia were enjoying a simple lunch of sandwiches and chips when Alex pulled into the driveway. His black SUV looked out of place parked next to their station wagon. He slid out of his front seat. His cane hit the ground before his feet. He was dressed warmly even though it was August. He made his way up to the front door and knocked.

Melissa emerged from the hallway and ran to the door. She opened it in a hurry.

"Hey!" she said, opening the door and stepping outside. She closed the door part way behind her. It made Jack very curious that Alex was not invited into the house. Melissa had been strangely passive all morning, and even though he appreciated her new found attitude, something wasn't right. He laid his sandwich down and walked over to the door.

"Daddy?" Olivia spoke up.

"I'll be right back," Jack said in a hurry.

As he approached the door, he could tell they were discussing the egging that took place the night before. He could hear Melissa clearly.

"I don't know who would have done this," Melissa said with a slight sense of panic, "or what this could mean."

"Let's not worry about it; everything's going to turn out fine. You just take care of that family of yours," Alex said. He did not seem worried.

Jack opened the door and stepped outside. "Is everything all right?" he asked.

"Yeah, everything's fine, Jack. Melissa was just telling me about the unfortunate situation with the eggs last night," Alex said. "It's a pity, your first night here and it looks like someone decided to have some fun with the new neighbors."

"Yeah, It was no big deal, more a nuisance," Jack said calmly, "I was more surprised by it. I didn't think things like that happened in Singleton."

Everyone was silent. It may have only been a few seconds, but it felt like an hour. Jack seemed to have struck a chord with his last comment. He didn't mean anything by it; he was just making a passing comment. Alex looked at him disapprovingly, like he took it personally. He took a deep breath through his nostrils. Melissa stared at her father, knowing that he was displeased. She looked at him anxiously, wondering what would be said next.

Alex finally broke the silence, "Well, let's not let a few bad apples spoil the whole bunch." He was calm, but Jack could tell he was displeased.

Jack tried to change the conversation, "Right, I'm not going to let it put a damper on our first days here. After lunch Olivia and I were going to check out the park up the road."

"Jack, you promised you would start on the lawn today!" Melissa interjected.

"Yeah, I know, but Olivia was really looking forward to the park, and we were waiting till after lunch. I'll just do it after we get back. We won't be long."

"Jack, please, I'd like you to get started on this right away. Olivia can wait, besides this will give her something to look forward to later this week."

Jack didn't want to fight right now, especially after things had been going so well between them all morning. Even though he was backing down yet again, he thought it would be the right thing to do. "All right, I'll see what I can do."

Melissa nodded approvingly. She continued, "Dad and I are going into town for a few hours. I will probably be back in time for dinner, but if not there's some pasta in the pantry you can cook."

Jack hated being bossed around these days, but at this point he felt he didn't have a choice, "All right, well, you have a good time."

"Thanks, Jack," Alex said with a smile. He began to turn away.

"Oh, one more thing," Jack stopped him, "Did your movers find anything in our trailer before returning it? Olivia swears she is missing an old shoebox of hers, and she didn't know if maybe your guys threw it out, or maybe put it somewhere."

"Can't say that they did," Alex said nonchalantly, "Tell her to keep looking, Jack, it may turn up." With that Alex turned and walked down the steps to his SUV.

"All right, I'll see you later, Jack," Melissa said. He opened the door for her to grab her purse right inside the doorway. She quickly grabbed it and headed down the steps toward the SUV.

"Have fun, be back before curfew," Jack said joking. Melissa turned giving him a half-smile. Jack couldn't believe how cordial Melissa was with him. Maybe this move to Singleton would work out after all. Jack was always hoping that they could quickly get things settled in their marriage, and then maybe move back to Denver someday. He could only dream that this stay in Singleton would be a short stint.

Jack returned to the table where Olivia was still sitting. She wasn't eating, just looking out the window like she had been watching her mother and grandfather drive off.

"Daddy, where are Mom and Grandpa going?"

"I'm not totally sure, Dear, they said something about checking out some shops and meeting some old friends."

"Why don't they like us?"

"What are you talking about, Olivia?" Jack knew full well what she was talking about. Melissa seemed far closer to her father lately than her own family. Jack more wondered why this came up now.

"Grandpa didn't even want to see me when he came. He doesn't like me or even care about me."

"Olivia, come on!" Jack said, trying to stifle the conversation. He knew that what Olivia was saying was at least partially true.

Olivia didn't say anything in response. Jack feared that she would feel like he was taking Alex's side. He felt like he needed to reassure her. "Look, I'm sorry, he should have come in, but maybe he was in a hurry. I don't know, sometimes Grandpa doesn't do a very good job of thinking about others. I'm sorry, Olivia, I don't know what to do."

She was still silent.

He continued, "How about this, why don't you relax this afternoon, maybe look for your box, watch some TV..."

"Daddy, I know Grandpa took my box. He made the men do it."

"All right, Olivia, we're done for now! I want you to go to your room, and we will talk about this later," Jack said slightly angry.

"But, Daddy!"

"No, I don't want to hear it right now. Let's just take a time-out, and we'll talk later."

"Ok," Olivia said, leaving her plate at the table, "Daddy?"

"Yes, Dear?"

"Can we still go to the park later?"

"Sure."

Chapter 8

Jack spent the afternoon working in the front yard. There were a few weeds to be pulled and some bushes to be trimmed. He didn't mind the work. Before they adopted Olivia, one of Jack's hobbies had been lawn care. He enjoyed working not only on his own yard, but others' as well. Over time it had become another source of income for the family. In Singleton Jack was determined to just do the bare minimum on the yard. He wanted to spend most of his time working on his marriage.

It was 4:30 in the afternoon when Olivia finally came outside. She found her Dad trimming the front bushes. She was still a little upset at how the day was unfolding. "Dad, can you please take me to the park soon? I've been waiting for such a long time and we may not have enough time if we don't go now!"

"Olivia, I'm almost done. You just need to be patient. Let me finish up with this and we will be on our way."

"But, Dad, Mom might be back soon and she won't want us to leave and…"

"I just need a few more minutes out here and then we can head out," Jack said with frustration in his voice.

Olivia knew that any further arguing was in vain. Her dad was living in fear of her mother, and this upset her. She wished that he would stand his ground to her more than he did. She thought her dad was right most of the time and that her mother had no business treating him the way she did. Right now she was making him do this yard work and keeping them from exploring Covington Park.

Covington was only two blocks from their house. It was located at the foot of Westwood Mountain. The fact that it was called a mountain was laughable. It was more like an oversized hill. The park looked interesting, but that was because it was surrounded by woods. It was a place that would definitely interest Olivia. She felt like it almost gave her an audible invitation to come and explore. Jack didn't know much about the park but thought it could be a place where he and Olivia could have some good father-daughter moments.

He worked until 5:30 in the evening when Olivia came out again. He had become preoccupied with organizing the small shed in their backyard. He didn't have any tools in the shed yet; first he wanted to clear all the spider webs out and repair a few loose boards in the floor. At times Jack was a perfectionist. He knew that if he didn't repair these boards now, it would be a lot harder after he moved all of his tools into the building.

"Dad, we need to go soon or it will be too late!" Olivia said approaching her dad.

"Olivia, you have got to calm down. Can't you see I'm in the middle of something?" Jack said, hoping she took notice of the wood boards pulled up.

"Daddy, you said we could go soon and Mom might be home any minute..."

"Olivia, it is not a big deal. Listen, we will just have to go tomorrow."

"But you start your job tomorrow!"

"We can go when I get home." Olivia did not like this answer because her mother was always discouraging her from exploring unknown areas and so far in this new town it seemed like her mother wanted to have her and Jack on an even tighter leash than before.

"Daddy, please can we go now!"

Jack was very frustrated at this moment. "Olivia, I want you to go inside. I need to finish this up. We can easily go to the park tomorrow when I get home, and if for some reason it doesn't work, then we can go the next day. It'll be ok."

Olivia left without saying a word and went back into the house. Jack could tell that she was upset. He started back on his work. Looking at the shed he saw the loose boards lying outside the building along with many of the tools. Jack felt horrible. He knew that Olivia had been looking forward to checking out Covington Park all day. He also knew that deep down inside he was letting Melissa control him. He was trying to appease her by working extra hard on the yard as well as getting the shed finished. The situation put Jack in such a conundrum; if he tried to please Melissa then Olivia would be upset, and likewise any attempt to go out of his way for Olivia would end up upsetting Melissa. In this case Jack knew that he should take Olivia to the park. He decided to quickly finish up his work in order to at least let Olivia see the park.

It took him about forty-five minutes to put the boards back and to move the tools into their places. Melissa was not home yet, so Jack thought he'd better hurry because Melissa probably would not want them to go. He quickly ran into the house calling for his daughter, "Olivia! Olivia! I got done a little early." He heard no answer. "Olivia! You still want to go to Covington?" He approached her room. He thought she was probably mad at him and he would need to do a bit of apologizing before they left.

He knocked on the door of her room, "Olivia, you in there?" He knocked again and heard nothing. He opened the door, "Olivia?"

She was gone!

$$\mathfrak{S}$$

He knew exactly where she was. She had been looking forward to visiting Covington Park since they arrived yesterday, and even before that Jack had told her that they were going to live near a park. He had originally told her about the park in order to make the move easier on her. He thought it would give her something to look forward to, but now he regretted ever mentioning it to her.

Even though the park was only a couple of blocks away he decided he would drive over to it. He was not exactly sure how large the park was. If there were roads that ran through it, then he could probably search the whole area quickly, but knowing Olivia, she was probably exploring the surrounding woods, especially because she knew the rumors that there might be caves in the woods. He was not worried about Olivia as much as he was mad. She knew better than to run off like this.

Jack quickly drove the few blocks to the park. He wanted to hurry as he didn't want Melissa to know anything about this incident. She would definitely rant about him being an irresponsible parent. He drove past the wooden sign into the heavily wooded park. Driving past the trees along the entry road, he came upon some old playground equipment next to a picnic area. There were trees everywhere which is quite unusual for western Illinois. It made the park look very dark.

Jack drove behind some of the playground equipment where he found a little parking area. He quickly parked his car and climbed out. There were no other cars in the area and it seemed that Jack was the only one there. He wondered how he would ever find Olivia. He looked in all directions. The only open area was a small baseball field that had not been well kept. It was all grown over with weeds. This seemed like a forgotten park.

Where should he begin looking? Olivia could be anywhere. As much as he disliked the folks of Singleton he wished there were some families around who had seen which direction she went. She couldn't have been there for more than half an hour, so she couldn't have made it far.

Jack's mind began to wonder. Even though Singleton had a great reputation, the thought of abduction did cross his mind. Maybe some wanderer came in from a neighboring town and was camping in the woods. Or maybe some college drinkers were out partying for the weekend and decided to play some sort of strange prank on a twelve-year-old girl. Jack would have had many other theories play through his head if they hadn't been interrupted.

To his left, about a hundred feet away, he saw a figure emerging from the woods. He could tell it was a little girl no more than five feet in height. She was coming from a spot that was grown over with bushes and vines. He knew right away that it was Olivia. Jack quickly ran to her calling out, "Olivia!"

Jack reached her just as she was getting her foot unstuck from the last bush. He was full of mixed emotions as he was both relieved that Olivia seemed unharmed and frustrated by the fact that she left in the first place. "Olivia, are you okay?"

"Yeah, I'm fine, Dad." Olivia seemed very stoic, as if lost in another world.

"Listen, you know better than to run off like that. You had me worried sick. What if you had gotten lost? What if someone had hurt you? It will be getting dark before long and if you were out here by yourself, what would you have done?"

Olivia was silent. She just stood there in front of Jack not making eye contact. Something was obviously wrong.

"Olivia, do you have anything to say for yourself?" Jack said wanting an apology from her.

"Daddy, I'm sorry, I just want to go home," Olivia responded, not wanting to argue at all. This caught Jack off guard. Usually Olivia's personality was strong enough that she would at least try to give some type of explanation for her behavior. Jack sensed that there was something deeper going on in her mind. Could this still be related to her box somehow? Maybe she found it in her room and was embarrassed so she sought to hide it. It sounded odd, but Jack had a variety of wild theories going through his mind.

"Well, let's head for the car, and you will be grounded for the rest of the week."

"Ok," Olivia answered very solemnly, not even making eye contact. In Jack's mind there was no question that something was wrong. He wondered what it could be.

"Olivia, are you all right?"

"Yeah, Dad, I'm fine, let's just go."

They both walked to the car without saying a word. It started raining ever so slightly. Olivia got in and quickly put on her seat belt. Jack fired up the engine as the rain started coming down heavier. He turned on the wipers. As he pulled out of the parking space and started for the park exit he glanced over at Olivia who was staring out the passenger side window. He noticed a few tears coming down her cheeks.

♋

Once at home Olivia headed straight to her room without even being told. Jack stood outside his daughter's door listening to her cry. This had been going on for about an hour now. It was an even steady cry, which was odd. Olivia had always been a tough young girl, and for her to be crying this much was unusual. She had always been prone to playing rough, and Jack and Melissa were used to the perpetual scraping of knees and bloodied lips.

But this cry was different. It had a sense of mystery behind it. Jack wondered, *What could have happened today?* This was not the cry of an injury or a cry of sorrow for disobeying her father.

Olivia had always had a spirit of independence about her; always looking to explore and discover new things. She had always been a sort of tomboy, and these woods definitely lent themselves to exploration.

The woods at Covington Park were thick, and the talk of hidden caves was too enticing for Olivia. The park proved to be nothing special and Jack knew that Olivia hadn't spent any time on the few pieces of play equipment or the overgrown baseball field. She was exploring the woods the whole time she was there.

Something happened in those woods earlier that day and Jack was determined to figure out what transpired. Olivia was the toughest twelve-year-old girl he knew, and for her to cry like this was definitely peculiar. Finally Jack had

had enough–he couldn't take the crying anymore. He was determined to figure out what was wrong with Olivia.

The door creaked as it opened into the dark room. The way the door opened brought light right onto the bed, seemingly putting a spot light on Olivia. Her face was stuffed into the pillow. Her muffled cry could still easily be heard.

Jack walked quietly over to the side of her bed and had a seat. "Olivia, are you ready to talk about what happened today?"

Jack waited for a response, but all he heard was Olivia's muffled cry.

"Did you hurt yourself?"

No response.

"Were there some kids at the park that hurt you?"

No response.

"Listen, Olivia, if we are going to make this new life work here, you have to talk to me…. please."

Olivia's crying eased up just a bit. She picked her head up just enough to wipe her eyes and nose.

Jack reached over to her dresser and grabbed her a couple of tissues. She took them, giving him a faint "Thank you."

"Now, are you ready to tell me what happened today at the park? Did something happen while you were in the woods?"

Jack didn't even have to ask her if she went anywhere else in the park. He knew his daughter well enough to know she was in the woods.

"Dad, I don't think I can," she said in between sniffs.

"Please, Honey, let's talk this through, you know you can tell me anything." Jack had always been a tender man, always talking to his daughter with deep affection in his voice.

"Dad, I can't, I really don't think I can," she said burying her head back into her pillow.

"Fine, when you are ready to talk, you come find me and tell me what happened today," Jack said, standing up with frustration in his voice.

He walked briskly over to door, and opened it rather hastily. The outside light poured in with the creaking of the door.

"Dad!" he heard as he opened the door.

He stopped just as he was about to walk out.

"Yes, Dear," said Jack, stepping back into the room and half way closing the door.

"It's not necessarily what happened today in the woods..." said Olivia trailing off.

"Then what is it?"

"It's not what happened in the woods, but it's what I saw."

Chapter 9

Jack could not get another word out of Olivia. It was as if she shut down after telling him she saw something. Maybe she thought twice about what she had already told her father and she digressed immediately. Jack tried and tried to pry any information he could from her but it was to no avail, and the crying became stronger and stronger. It was getting late into the evening when he thought he would give it one more try to get some information out of his daughter. Jack entered her room again, determined for results.

"Olivia, listen…"

Olivia turned her head away from Jack to face the wall. The crying became stronger.

"I can help you with this. Maybe tomorrow evening you can take me to your spot and show me what you saw. I want to…" Jack was interrupted mid-thought. The front door of the house opened and slammed shut. Melissa was home. Olivia picked her head up from the pillow and looked straight at Jack with wide eyes.

"Daddy, quick, I don't want her to see me."

"What?" Jack said, totally dumbfounded.

"Please, keep her out of here," Olivia said in a whisper, "Don't let her see me crying."

"Jack!" Melissa called out loudly from the living room.

"Please, Daddy!" Olivia pleaded with her father.

Jack didn't know what to do, but he was sympathetic to his daughter's request. He could tell there was urgency in her voice, and he wanted to do whatever he could to protect her. He quickly exited the bedroom and gently shut the door behind him. Even though it was eight o'clock, maybe Melissa would think Olivia was asleep.

Jack walked to the living room to find Melissa putting her purse down on the table. He could tell she was looking for food and was wondering what he and Olivia had for dinner. "Did you hear me call you? Where were you?" she asked slightly irritated.

"I was just looking after Olivia, she's in bed," he responded, not even making eye contact. He thought it all sounded suspicious coming out of his mouth.

"Already in bed? It's just past eight!" she said, puzzled. Olivia had always been somewhat of a night owl and the thought of her catching an early bedtime had to sound just a little off.

"Yeah, I don't think she is feeling well. You know, all the excitement of this new place, and we did a lot outside today; she's probably just a little overwhelmed. I'm sure she'll get over it, but anyway how was your day?" Jack really didn't care about hearing what she did with her father, but he was looking desperately to change the subject.

"It was fine," Melissa responded. She seemed anxious to inform Jack of some new business around the town. "Jack, sorry I was later than expected in getting home. This egging of our house has got some of the residents around town worried. We don't want to cause any trouble here and we don't want the residents thinking that we are to blame in some way for this. I mean, what if this continues around town because of something we did?"

You have got to be kidding me, thought Jack, *we just moved from Denver. I don't even think the police would come out for a house egging.*

He spoke up, "Melissa, it's probably just a stupid egging. Some kid was picking on the new folks. I don't see what the big deal is."

"Jack, I don't understand you. Someone vandalized our home, and you just want to sit around here and do nothing about it. What kind of man are you? Stop thinking about yourself and think of your daughter for once."

Melissa knew how to push Jack's buttons, and she was in no mood to hold back. Jack would usually counter her mean-spiritedness or try to at least defend himself, but at this moment he thought otherwise. He kept thinking of Olivia crying in bed. His mind was definitely focused on her and he was not in the mood to spar with Melissa. Ultimately he didn't care what the people of Singleton thought. They were too self-absorbed and obsessed with their town, and Melissa was falling right in line with them. All he wanted at the moment was to be reassured that his daughter was going to be okay.

"Yeah, I see what you mean, Melissa. We don't want people egging our house or something like that." It sounded so insincere coming out of his mouth.

"Jack, it's like you're not even trying. We want to build this new life in Singleton. If you want to become a part of this town, you will need to help out with this effort."

"Effort?"

"Yes, to catch the criminal," Melissa said emphatically, "We can't have criminals carelessly roaming our streets. This is Singleton after all."

In that moment Jack feared for the boy he saw the other night. If he was the perpetrator, the shame on his family and the punishment he would face would be incredible. He tried to appease Melissa, "All right, well, I'll keep my eyes open. It'll be all right, Dear. I imagine it's just some kid looking for a cheap thrill. I imagine folks will figure out what is going on and everything will work itself out. I wouldn't worry about a thing."

"Well, that's all I need, just the reassurance that we are going to work together on things like this." Melissa seemed calmed by Jack's response. He gave her a small kiss on the top of her forehead. She nuzzled up close to him as he embraced her with a small hug. Even though things in Singleton had started off very strange, at least at this moment he was hugging his wife. This would not have seemed like much to any other couple, but for the Averys this had become a rarity. Maybe moving to Singleton was a sacrifice that would pay off in the long run. Jack could only hope.

♋

It was late. Jack couldn't sleep. The events of the day once again kept him awake. What was going on with Olivia? What did she see in the woods? Did his short embrace with Melissa mean anything? Was she finally changing back to the Melissa of old? What would become of the kid who egged their home? All these questions seemed to pass through Jack's mind. It was approaching midnight. He was sitting alone on his couch.

Just like many other nights lately when he couldn't sleep he decided to read his Bible. This was basically the only time he ever read his Bible outside of church. Ever since meeting Melissa, his spiritual life had begun to gradually slip. Melissa, for the most part, never took an interest in Jack's spiritual life or church, and Jack got out of the habit of regular Bible reading. Tonight he would read of Christ's sacrifice, giving Himself for the world's sins. Jack's father always said that God showed his love to the world by the sacrifice of Christ; Jesus died in our place, he would say.

As a boy, Jack became obsessed with the theme of sacrifice in the Bible. He would often read the odd story of Abraham attempting to sacrifice his son Isaac but being stopped at the last minute by God. He never quite fully understood it, but just the idea of the story fascinated him.

This was Jack's late night reading. These stories were a comfort to him. He thought of how his Dad read them to him and his brother. Of course Steve, his brother, took these stories to heart and later he went on to enter the ministry as a pastor. Even though Jack's family thought he wasn't listening, Jack was actually taking in every world. These stories from the Bible were an anchor to him during life's difficulties and struggles, and now while this new life in Singleton was presenting its own struggles, Jack felt like he needed God in his life more than ever.

He decided to pray. "God, I need you! I don't know what's going on, but I need your help. I feel like I'm either losing my wife or my child. Help Olivia! I don't know what is going on. I'm so confused. Was she harmed? What's wrong with her? You have to help me out in some way. I just don't know what to do. Please, just give me some sort of sign or anything! How am I supposed to…"

Jack was interrupted. He heard another crack against his front door. It startled him but he knew right away what it was. He quickly rose from the couch and raced toward the front door. This time he didn't have any fear. He quickly opened the door and saw what he expected. More eggs! Once again, the runny yolks were coming down his front windows onto his porch. More than frustrated, he was puzzled by the question of why this was happening. What did he or his family ever do to make someone want to do this?

He stood staring at the mess on his house when his mind went to the kid who did it. Jack wasn't angry or vengeful toward him, rather he feared for his safety. He thought of the boy he saw the other night. If this kid did do this, then he deserved to be punished, but not the way the town would punish him. Jack wondered if he could see the kid up the road as he did the night before.

Jack ran down the steps and indeed saw the same teenage boy standing a little more than a hundred yards up the road. He was dressed basically the same as the night before, and he was looking straight at Jack. At that moment something else caught Jack's eye. A man jumped out of a parked gold Suburban situated a few feet from Jack's property. The man was nicely dressed like he was some sort of a private investigator on a mission. He took off running toward the boy.

The teenage kid saw what was transpiring and decided to flee the scene. He didn't run up the road but rather through someone's yard. The kid disappeared into the backyard of a local resident. Dogs began to bark and Jack could see a couple of neighbors' inside lights turn on. The supposed investigator didn't stop, but continued the same route the boy ran, and in a few seconds both were gone from Jack's sight.

He stood dumbfounded at the thought of what just happened. He asked himself, "Did I really just see that?" Everything calmed down very quickly. It was apparent that someone had been watching his house, waiting for this kid. Why was it so important? Was this someone the town knew as a menace? Were the people of Singleton waiting for a reason to prosecute this kid? Still a bigger question remained, "Why did this kid strike the same house two nights in a row?" Did he really hate new folks in town this much? Or was there something deeper in this egging? Maybe there truly was some sort of dispute with Melissa from the past that had never been resolved. Maybe this kid was doing a favor for an old boyfriend of hers or something like that. Jack was determined to ask Melissa about it in the morning. The more he thought about it, the more he convinced himself that Melissa was holding some important information from him.

As if someone had just snapped their fingers, Jack's mind raced back into reality. He thought about running after the boy and the investigator, but then thought twice. He really didn't want to get involved in the drama of Singleton, and besides the front of his house was still covered in eggs. Jack quickly cleaned up the mess and headed back inside.

The latest egging did not faze him as much as the first. After all of the strange events that had occurred since they arrived, Jack was exhausted and just ready to start his first work week. He quietly snuck into his bedroom and slipped into bed. Melissa didn't budge. He'd rather not discuss the egging with her at this moment. She was sleeping so soundly and he was ready to do the same.

As Jack laid his head on the pillow he remembered that he was praying before he was interrupted. He felt that he needed a little closure in his time with God. He whispered a little prayer, "Help me, God, this is a crazy place."

Chapter 10

Jack sat at the desk in his office, bored out of his mind. It was Thursday and his first work week had left a lot to be desired. His job at *Singleton Software Design* was as quiet as they come. Upon arriving on Monday, he was assigned to the customer care department. His job was to answer calls from local customers concerning technical questions. So far for the week, he had answered three calls. Two of them took less than two minutes, and the other just over five. He started to feel like this was a job that Alex had someone in the company create specifically for him. It was totally useless.

The worst part was there was another guy already assigned to the position. They shared the same cubicle and sat only a few feet from each other. It was Melissa's cousin, Gus, a forty-three year old single, overweight man who basically ate all day. He constantly had food or some type of sauce stuck in his large mustache. He talked nonstop to Jack throughout the whole day, most of the time with his mouth full of food. His usual topics of conversation included the weather, sports, people in Singleton, the local café's food, and his family. Jack heard extensively about all the members of his family and what each of Gus' five siblings were doing in Singleton. He had already told Jack three times about his brother who died shortly after birth. It was obviously something that was heavy on his mind.

Gus was currently carrying on about the sandwiches at the local café. "The meat has never been real fresh on the Reuben. It tastes like it was something from last week, but if you get enough special sauce for it, it tastes just like the Philly deluxe..." By now Jack had learned how to tune Gus out and just let him talk. He would be a somewhat likeable guy if one didn't have to spend eight hours a day with him. The chatter was so excessive that Jack didn't know how he was going to make it through the rest of week, much less months of this.

He looked up at the clock; it was approaching eleven in the morning. Jack usually brought his lunch to work but today he really wanted to get away from it all. He thought he would check out the local café. Even though he knew it would be filled with folks from the town, he very much needed a break from Gus.

Gus continued, "Then there was Betty Louise, who has never been quite right after the incident with the baseball bat," he had moved on to discuss the latest gossip around town, "she just ain't right. They got to keep people watching her house constantly for fear that she might hurt someone or maybe even herself." Jack had already heard about Betty Louise a few times and he didn't feel like discussing her any more.

Looking up at the clock, Jack once more decided to change the subject, "Gus, do you mind if I take an early lunch? I've got some hunger pains, if you know what I mean." Jack stood up and pushed his chair under his desk, "Anything you recommend at the café?"

"It all sort of tastes the same to me. I'd just get whatever's on special, you can't go wrong."

"All right, well, thanks Gus. I'll see you after a while," Jack left before Gus could respond. His supervisor didn't seem to care about Jack or Gus, so Jack thought taking an early lunch break would not be an issue. He left without speaking to anyone on his way out. He hopped into his station wagon and headed back toward the small downtown area of Singleton. *Singleton Software Design* was located on the edge of town so it would take him just under ten minutes to arrive at the café.

On the drive over, he thought about skipping lunch altogether and heading home to check on Olivia. She hadn't been the same since last Sunday, the day she ventured off into the woods in Covington Park. Her demeanor was subdued, and she did not feel like talking much with her father or mother. It was a total mystery. Jack had even stopped by the park a couple of times to see if there was anything strange happening or something that would possibly give him a clue. He found nothing that gave him a hint of what Olivia saw. He was thankful that through it all he was able to keep this hidden from Melissa. Olivia had insisted on it, and he was going to honor his daughter and keep this from his wife.

It was a beautiful day in Singleton. On his drive he saw kids playing and parents walking with their children. Jack always thought the adults in town never looked like they were enjoying themselves. They seemed too serious, like life was all business. He thought maybe their love and patriotism for the town had driven them into a subdued way of looking at life. He was determined to never become like that. It looked like a miserable way to live.

He pulled up to the café and the parking lot was already half full, even though it was just past eleven. It was a simple looking café, a stand-alone building. It looked like it could hold about fifty customers if it was absolutely packed. Jack had never eaten there, but he really wanted to venture out and try something new, anything to have a few minutes away from Gus. He parked his car and entered the café.

Upon entering there were about twenty-five folks sitting at booths, tables and the bar. The restaurant didn't come to complete silence, but many of the people stopped to stare. It was obvious that Jack was the "new guy" in town. He walked over to one of the corner booths and took a seat. Slowly the folks went back to their meals and conversations without paying attention to Jack. He grabbed the menu propped up on the table and began reading, trying to pretend he didn't notice people occasionally staring at him.

A middle-aged waitress walked over to take his order. "What would you like," seemingly not in the mood to make much conversation with him.

"What's the special for today?"

"Beef burger with fries."

"What's a beef burger?" Jack said, puzzled.

"It's the same as a hamburger, it's just loose ground beef put on a bun, you know what I'm sayin'?" the waitress responded. Jack could sense a little irritation in her voice.

"Well that sounds good to me," he said trying to sound upbeat.

"What would you like on it?"

"I'll have it with everything, whatever comes on it."

"If you say so," the waitress said, walking away. Jack sat looking out the window to his left. Beautiful days like this one made him want to be home, back in Denver. He enjoyed all the outdoor activities he and Olivia would do together. He thought of taking her fishing, and maybe some quiet time by a lake would be just what was needed to open her up. Between his job and Olivia not being herself, this week seemed to be going by at a snail's pace.

Looking out the window, Jack saw a pay phone located at the edge of the parking lot. The phone line at his house was still not set up and the cell phone tower hadn't been fixed which Jack thought was very strange. He was anxious to hear from home and made a mental note to be sure to call home before he left. He wanted to hear from his brother Steve more than anything. They did everything together and always had until this present move to

Singleton. Jack fished in his pocket and made sure he had the correct change to make the call.

The waitress arrived back with his large beef burger with everything on it including jalapeños. "You didn't tell me what you wanted to drink, so I brung you some ice water," she said sounding a bit upset.

"Thank you very much, it looks great," Jack responded.

♋

After eating his beef burger and taking a few minutes to relax, he headed back to work. He had been gone for just over an hour. Before leaving the parking lot, he called his brother Steve from the pay phone. No one answered so he left a message. Steve was always a great encouragement for him. It seemed like Steve always knew the right thing to say at the right moment. Though Jack was older, Steve seemed to be a steady anchor for him. Steve was just a step ahead of him in almost every area of life. This didn't make him jealous of Steve, but rather Jack adored him. It was very hard not to be able to talk with him during this difficult and strange first week in Singleton.

As Jack was driving back to work he thought of the boy who egged his house. He assumed the boy was not caught by the man chasing him. He never heard anything more about the incident and his house had stayed egg-free since then. He asked Melissa about it, but she had no more information about why this might be happening. Jack hoped that he had seen the last of eggs on the front of his house, and that this whole thing was just some kid that wanted to "welcome" the new residents of Singleton.

Upon pulling back into the *Singleton Software Design* parking lot, Jack could see his supervisor waiting outside. He looked angry. He was standing a few spaces from Jack's parking space. He was a very tall man, standing no shorter than six feet, five inches. His legs made up most of his height, and part of his bare legs could be seen in between his socks and his pants. Jack imagined that finding pants to fit his long legs was probably no easy task. He wore thick glasses and his shirts were always buttoned to the top button, but with no tie. One would think that this man tried his hardest to play the part of an office nerd.

Jack pulled into his parking space and waited a second or two before exiting his car. He was the first to speak, "Stewart, how are you doing?" He said, trying to sound pleasant.

"Jack, you know you're only supposed to take half an hour for lunch. What were you doing?"

This was the first time Stewart had ever pursued Jack to discuss basically anything. Jack had gone out of his way a few times to speak with him but this was a different confrontation all together. "Things were slow at the desk and Gus seemed to have everything under control, so I thought I would just step out and grab a quick bite to eat."

Stewart was not satisfied. "Jack, I don't care what kind of day it is; you are not to leave your desk. Like we discussed, you have a thirty minute lunch break and that is to be taken at your desk. You do not leave *Singleton Software Design* until the day is over. Do you understand?"

Jack was so emotionally detached from his job that he didn't mind challenging his employer, "Listen, Stewart, there was no harm done. I just stepped out to get a quick bite to eat. There was..."

Stewart interrupted him, "Jack, if you don't know by now, we had to pull some strings to get you this job. You better see that you appreciate it. As easy as it was to bring you on, we can cut you off too."

Jack was tired of fighting. "Ok, I won't let it happen again," he said with a slow, gentle nod toward Stewart.

"All right, well go ahead and get back to work, and don't ever do this again."

Jack entered the building and headed toward his office area. Gus was lounging in his chair with his legs stretched out. His arms were folded and his head was against his chest. He had fallen asleep and by the large wet area of drool by the collar of his shirt, it looked like he had been asleep since the time Jack left. He decided to wake him.

"So did I miss anything? How many calls did you get?" Jack said loudly. Gus was startled by the loud voice and quickly gathered himself. He sat up in his chair and adjusted his glasses.

"What was that?" he said wiping the drool from his chin.

"Oh, did you receive any calls?"

"Nah, I don't figure as much, I kind of just dozed off to tell you the truth."

♋

It had been a long day for Jack. Gus continued discussing his usual topics with him. They didn't receive any calls for the rest of the day. It turned out to be another long day of watching the clock roll by and trying to tune out Gus. As he drove home, Jack couldn't believe that he would have to do this all over again in under twenty-four hours. The thought made him a little sick. It was on this drive home that Jack seriously considered the idea of moving back to Denver. He had wondered before if moving here was a mistake, but now he realized that he couldn't take too much more of this adventure in Singleton. A lot of times he saw Olivia as his only escape from the pressures of life, but now even that was taken from him. She hadn't been herself the last few days. He knew that something had to change and change quickly.

Jack pulled into his driveway. He was glad to be home but already dreading another day of work tomorrow. He gathered his things out of his car and entered the house. Once inside, he found Melissa and Olivia silently eating a homemade meal. He was annoyed by the fact that Melissa didn't bother to wait for him for dinner. He had to get gas on the way home which ended up making him just a few minutes late. The station was a little out of the way. Jack decided to let the whole thing go and not fight with Melissa.

"Hey, how's it going? What's for dinner?" Jack said, trying to cheerful.

"Chicken," Melissa responded matter-of-factly.

"Sounds good," Jack responded, setting his work bag on the floor. "Did you save me any?"

"It's in the kitchen."

Jack walked over to the kitchen to find the casserole sitting on the stove. He grabbed a plate and took a large helping. He walked over to the dining room and sat in between Melissa and Olivia.

"So, how was your day?" he said, aiming the question at Melissa.

No response.

"Anything new happen today?" Jack said, sensing that something was wrong.

Melissa spoke up, "Olivia, Sweetie, would you mind going to your room?"

Olivia got up from the table without saying a word. She took both her plate and her silverware. As soon as the door to her room slammed shut, Melissa started in on him.

"Jack, I heard the news today that you left work without permission and took an extra long lunch break. I can't believe you!"

"Melissa, what in the world is going on? It's no big deal, and how do you know about all this?"

"Word travels fast in a small town. We are new in this town and you are ruining our reputation by the minute."

Jack quickly became frustrated, "Melissa, I don't care about any sort of reputation we have in this town. Who cares what people think?"

Melissa stood up, "Jack Avery! Did you hear me? We are new in this town, and we want to fit in as much as possible. If you keep acting up like this, we will never be accepted by the people here."

Jack threw his napkin down and stood up to match Melissa's intensity, "I did not do anything wrong. I was hungry and went out for a bite to eat, nothing more!"

"*Singleton Software Design* is an important company and one where you can't just do whatever you want. You aren't the boss anymore, Jack! What if something had happened and they needed you while you were gone?" Melissa said, stepping a little too close to Jack.

"Nothing was happening at work!" Jack shouted. He was out of control at this point, "I was sitting around listening to Gus talk about the food he likes, who he is related to, the story of his baby brother, random gossip about people around town," Jack stopped to take a breath, "I just couldn't take much more of it. He's so sloppy too. He chews with his mouth open and slobbers. He's a nice guy, but he needs help."

Melissa seemed to be taken aback by Jack's assertive attitude. She stood staring at him like she was trying to take in what he was saying. Jack thought she was offended by him talking about her cousin and tried to do some damage control, "Look, I'm sorry to talk about a family member in such a bad light, but he's been quite overbearing and..."

"No, you're right," Melissa interrupted. Her demeanor was completely changed, "I know he can be quite overbearing at times."

Jack couldn't believe what he was hearing. He just complained about someone in her family and she actually agreed with him. Usually she was pretty defensive about her family and to have her sympathize with his complaints was quite remarkable.

He continued on with more empathy in his voice, "Listen, don't get me wrong, I do like the guy. It's just hard listening to him day in and day out."

"Maybe it's because he lives alone and doesn't have anyone to talk to," Melissa said.

"Yeah, I think you're right. He tells me from time to time that this job is really all he has. There's not a whole lot for him to look forward to. He has worked there for over twenty years."

The rest of dinner went great. Olivia didn't return from her room, but Jack and Melissa were able to have a somewhat cordial conversation for the next half hour. In the back of his mind Jack was still thinking about moving back to Denver and was trying to decide when and how to bring it up to Melissa. He knew that it would have to be discussed at just the right time. He could see a major fight brewing if he brought it up prematurely.

Chapter 11

Jack awoke Friday morning and began his usual routine: shower, shave, breakfast. Since the previous evening, he and Melissa seemed to be on better terms. For the first time in a long time they were able to get through breakfast without a fight. Olivia, on the other hand, was still quiet and didn't say a word at breakfast. Ever since the "incident" at Covington Park she only spoke to her father at times of absolute necessity. He didn't know what was going on with her. What was she hiding from him? Before he left for work, Jack decided to give it another try to see if he could get anything out of her.

He knocked on her door, "Olivia?"

No answer.

"Olivia? Are you in there?"

Again no answer. He decided to go ahead and enter without waiting.

He found Olivia quietly sitting on her bed looking through some old camping gear. Jack loved taking her to parks around Denver. He figured they probably went camping or backpacking three or four times a year. Olivia was fiddling with an old head lamp he had given her soon after she was adopted. She was still in her pajamas and by the amount of equipment she had out it didn't look like she was going anywhere for a while.

"Dad, do you need something?" she said in a serious tone.

"No, I just thought I would check on you before I left for work."

"Well, I'm fine. I'm just looking through this stuff."

He walked over and sat on the end of the bed. Olivia didn't acknowledge him, but continued fiddling with her equipment. "Listen, if there is something you want to tell me, I'd be more than happy to hear it. I won't be mad, promise."

"No, I'm fine, Dad."

Jack decided to shoot straight. "Olivia, I can assure you I will not be mad if you tell me what happened the other day in Covington."

"Dad, it's fine, I think I just got a little spooked or something. I'm ok." She seemed so much older to him than just a few days before. She was even calling him 'Dad' as opposed to his usual title 'Daddy'. Jack felt like he was losing his little girl. They usually shared their thoughts with each other, but now there was something between them;

something he knew Olivia was holding back. This morning it did not appear that he was going to make any significant breakthrough.

"Well, how about this, over the weekend let's take some time and go fishing, just like we used to do at Cherry Creek? What do you say?"

"Sounds good, Dad," Olivia said, obviously just trying to appease her father.

"Ok, well, you be a good girl today," Jack said, getting up to leave. He was disappointed with how the conversation had gone, but he was thankful for the promise of a fishing trip. Hopefully they could have some quality father-daughter time which would allow Olivia to open up with him. Usually their fishing trips guaranteed at least one deep conversation between Jack and his daughter. He could only hope that this time would be no different.

♋

As Jack drove to work he thought more about what may have been in the woods at Covington. He wondered if maybe Olivia had stumbled upon some sort of drug exchange, but then he realized that something like that would not have spooked Olivia. She would have been brave enough to tell him about it. It was like there was something supernatural or magical about her experience in the woods. His mind wandered. It was almost as though Olivia had seen a ghost. After all the strange events that happened that first weekend, he would not put it past this town.

He thought back to the first time he saw Olivia majorly distressed. It was about three weeks after her adoption. After bringing Olivia home, the first few weeks went very smoothly for the Avery family. Olivia was very well behaved and respectful of her new parents. She even took great responsibility in her chores. It was very much the honeymoon stage of the adoption.

It was a Saturday afternoon, and Melissa had spent the morning grocery shopping. Jack and Olivia were spread out in their living room putting together a large model airplane when Melissa returned.

"Hey, guys, I'm home!" Melissa said, coming through the doors with her arms full of groceries.

"Hey, welcome home, how did everything go?" Jack responded.

"It went fine. I feel like I got enough food to last us a month. Jack, can you tell Olivia to start putting the groceries away? I've got a lot more in the car."

"She's right here, I'll let her know," Jack said looking at Olivia, making sure she heard. One of Olivia's chores around the house was helping her mother with the groceries, particularly helping to put them away when Melissa came home from the supermarket. Most of the time, Melissa was the one to do the shopping and Olivia usually wanted to help. Jack and Melissa thought this would be a great chore for Olivia, though right now she was preoccupied with the model airplane.

"Daddy, I don't want to put the groceries away. I want to stay with you and finish this airplane," Olivia protested to her father.

"Listen, it'll be ok. After you put the groceries away, we can get right back to work. I promise."

"But, Daddy, I don't want to do it!"

"Olivia, you know the rules!" Jack said, raising his voice, "Mom needs help. You go help Mom. I'm going to get a little cleaned up, but after you're done, come right back here and we can get back to work."

"Daddy, I just..."

"Olivia, I don't want to hear it. Go help Mom, and then we can get back to work."

Olivia stood up in frustration and headed for the kitchen. She was clearly upset. She was enjoying making the model airplane and didn't want to stop working on it. Jack figured she would cool off after a few minutes. Jack's hands had gotten rather messy working with the glue and paint and he thought he would try to get a little of it off before they started back working.

He was in their guest bathroom washing his hands when he heard Melissa cry out from the kitchen, "What are you doing?"

Jack quickly dried off his hands and headed to the kitchen in a hurry. What he found shocked him. Instead of putting the groceries away, Olivia had seen the groceries her mother had brought in and, in frustration, began throwing them against the refrigerator and pouring out the milk onto the floor. It looked like she'd already made it through a gallon before Melissa found her. The area was a mess.

Melissa clearly spoke with anger in her voice, "Olivia, you know better than this. You've never done anything like this before. What were you thinking?"

Olivia was crying just a little as she answered, "I just don't want to do this now. We need to finish the airplane."

Melissa continued, "I can't believe you would do this! Olivia, after all we've done for you. How could you have..."

"Ok, let's just cool down a minute," Jack said, trying to calm things down, "Melissa, if you wouldn't mind cleaning this up, I can deal with Olivia here and figure out an appropriate punishment." Melissa clearly did not like this suggestion, but figured it was probably best.

"Come with me, Olivia," Jack said sternly. He took her to the back bedroom and shut the door. He picked Olivia up and sat her on the bed.

Jack looked straight at his daughter, "Olivia, what was that all about? Why did you make that mess in the kitchen?" Olivia sat silently, looking down at her hands. She was crying harder at this point.

Jack sat beside her on the bed, "Olivia, to make this work we're going to have to talk to one another. What is going on?"

"I just don't know what to do," Olivia spoke through her tears. "Everything is so new. I kind of miss the nuns, and I just wanted to keep working on the airplane."

"Olivia, I understand that everything is so new, and there are lots of changes, but be assured that your mother and I love you very much. We're going to do all we can for you. You're our daughter and we will make any sacrifice for you. We love you!" He said, trying to reassure her.

"I know, Daddy, but I just…" Olivia broke off mid-sentence.

"Go ahead, Sweetie, you can tell me," Jack said gently patting his daughter on the back.

Olivia wiped some of her tears away, "I just hoped my family would come for me someday. I wanted to meet them and know who they were. Why did they leave me, Daddy?"

"Olivia, I'm sorry, and I don't know why they did what they did. I imagined you wanted to meet them someday, and maybe someday you will find them. I don't know anything about them or where they are, but maybe sometime when you are older we can try to locate them."

Jack handed her a tissue. She grabbed it and wiped her nose. She sat silently looking down at the used tissue. Her crying stopped just a bit. Jack continued, "Olivia, know this: that I love you so much and there is nothing you can do to change that. You're always going to be my daughter, and you're always going to be part of my life."

Olivia reached over and gave her father a hug, "Thank you, Daddy, I love you too." They sat for about a minute in silence. He wanted her to be reassured that he was not going anywhere and she could always depend on him. Jack held his daughter tightly.

"All right, Olivia, why don't we go and apologize to Mom together and help her clean up the mess, then we can finish the plane. How does that sound?"

"Sounds great, Daddy!"

This was a memory Jack clung to. It was the first moment of real tenderness he had with Olivia. It was at that point that Jack felt Olivia truly began to look at him as her father.

$$\text{♋}$$

Arriving at work, Jack took his normal parking spot. He was in no hurry as he was not looking forward to another day with Gus. What would be on his mind today? Jack was actually hoping his supervisor would see that two men working in customer care was not necessary. Gus actually loved the job and Jack would hate to take it away from the poor guy. Jack desired to be either transferred or fired. Being fired would actually have its advantages; it could be a way for Jack to open up the conversation to Melissa about moving back to Denver.

As Jack entered the office, he couldn't help but pick up on the stares from his coworkers. This was a normal routine for him as he entered work. He didn't know if he would ever break the perception of being the "new guy." He always knew that new-comers to Singleton were not truly welcomed, but he held out hope that things would change.

Upon arriving at his desk, he immediately realized something was different. He couldn't believe it. What was the meaning of this? This was something he never would have expected and it totally baffled Jack...there was no Gus!

Gus was always at work at least fifteen minutes early. He looked forward to his job and never took a day off. He was very loyal to the company and never had a harsh word to say about his supervisors. Jack wondered if everything was well with Gus. He must have been at least 100 pounds overweight, so Jack's first thought was a heart attack or some other sort of medical concern.

He quickly walked up the hall to his supervisor's office. Knocking on his door, Jack chuckled a little at the irony of his concern for Gus. Just yesterday he was struggling with the concept of having to face another day working alongside him, and now he was eager to figure out where he was.

"Come in!" Jack heard from inside the office.

He opened the door and found Stewart sitting behind his desk with his arms folded. It was almost as though he was expecting him. Jack decided to get right to the point, "Hey, where's Gus? Is everything all right?"

"Yes, everything's fine. He's not coming in today," Stewart said calmly.

"Why, what's going on?"

He leaned back in his chair, taking a deep breath through his nostrils, "He has actually been relieved of his duties."

"What?" Jack was stunned. This was not at all what he was expecting. Gus had been at the company for over twenty-five years. Why was he now being fired?

Stewart was calm and very matter-of-fact, "Yes, we didn't need two guys doing what you do, so we decided to cut one loose. We didn't need him."

Jack was angry at his cool attitude, "He's been at this company twenty-five years. He loved it here. What's he going to do?"

"Listen, Jack, you got to admit the guy was basically dead-weight. We didn't need him. It was a great time to get rid of him. Won't it be nice not to have that blabbing idiot talking your head off all day?"

Jack couldn't believe what he was hearing. True, Gus was overbearing at times, but at the end of the day he really was a nice guy who cared for others. Jack felt horrible about every mean thing he had ever said about the guy. He continued, "I don't know what to say, I know he thought a lot of you and..."

"Jack, are trying to make me feel bad? I don't need any sort of guilt trip from you. I've been at this company a long time, and by our profit margin I'd say I know what I'm doing. If you will excuse me, I have a lot of work to do."

Jack left the office like a defeated puppy. He felt so sorry for Gus. He wondered what Gus thought. Was he mad at Jack? Did he think that Jack got him fired? Jack felt nauseated at the idea of it. Was there some way he could rectify this situation?

Sitting back at his desk, he thought about the conversation he had the night before with Melissa. He felt very guilty about complaining to her about him, but yet he could not shake the idea that she was behind all of this. Her father obviously had enough influence in town to get him this job, so obviously he had enough power to get someone fired. The more Jack thought about this, the more he was certain of it. Even though getting Gus fired would be a despicable thing to do, he wouldn't put it past Melissa.

Jack arrived home later that day to find Olivia alone. She was sitting on the front porch when he arrived. She was dirty but this was not unusual. He was accustomed to her playing outside and exploring. What was odd was that her hands and knees were exceptionally dirty like she had been digging. She sat on the porch very complacently. Her red hair seemed to glow in the summer sun. Jack stared her over as he walked up their steps. He could tell she was hiding something from him.

"Olivia, what's with the mud?" He didn't even bother with a greeting.

"I don't know I just got carried away out there and got a little muddy," she said rubbing her hands together in an effort to minimize the mud. Jack was curious to hear more about where she had been, but for the moment his mind was stuck on idea of confronting Melissa about Gus being let go from his job.

"Ok, well, where is your mother, has she seen you?" He knew Melissa was not fond of Olivia's ways of playing rough.

"I'm not sure, she said she had a few errands to run but would probably return before you got home."

"Did she go with Grandpa?"

"Yes, he came and picked her up like he always does."

"What?" Jack had not realized that this had been a normal occurrence this past week. He wondered what was going on. Was there something Melissa was also hiding from him? Olivia didn't get a chance to explain anything because just then Alex pulled into the driveway, dropping off his daughter like she was a teenager at the movies. Jack hated Alex for this. He didn't even pretend to have a relationship with him or Olivia. Melissa got out of the SUV, grabbing her purse.

As she approached the front steps Jack was the first to speak, "Hey, what's up, where have you been?"

"I was just out with my father, running some errands. There are lots of people here that I want to see and catch up with."

Jack was angry with this answer. It was like Alex was rubbing off on her. Did she not think about Olivia? Why was she not taking Olivia with her? One would think that Melissa would be excited to show her daughter off to others. She did not realize how selfish she sounded. He didn't hold back, "Olivia told me you've been doing this every day. You've been going into town with your father."

She could tell he was angry. "Oh, calm down, Jack! Why do you care? I've got to do something to fill up my days."

Olivia excused herself and went into the house. Jack kept going, "Why was I not aware of any of this, and why have you been leaving Olivia here all by herself? Don't you think she would appreciate spending some time with you?"

Melissa was completely caught off guard by all of this. She was not one to take conversations like this lightly. "Olivia knows she can come with me whenever she wants," she said, pointing her finger into Jack's chest.

"Well, I'm sure she would appreciate it if you invited her every once in a while, and what's with you spending all this time with your father? I thought we moved here for us to reestablish our marriage and our family."

"Jack, you act like it is some crime for me to be out with my father. What is with you? I thought I would come home and find you in a good mood. I was hoping you had a better day than the last few."

"What is that supposed to mean?"

"I don't know; I just hoped that maybe since it is Friday or something that you would have had a much better day of work."

Jack realized that his speculations were correct, "So you did do it. You are responsible!"

"Responsible for what, Jack? You're talking like someone who's crazy."

"I'm talking about Gus. You are the reason he wasn't at work today. I knew you had something to do with this. Ever since we talked last night, you seemed like you were going to do something about him."

She realized she could not keep up the front. She might as well admit that she was indeed behind it all, "Come on, Jack! You were saying he was making your job miserable. I did you a favor. Now you can sit at work in peace without that slob bothering you with his nonsense throughout the day. I think everyone wanted him gone."

Jack was obviously upset and he was at the point of yelling, "It was all he had! He had worked there for over twenty years! What else is he going to do? Is he going to be all right?"

"Jack, why do you care? Yesterday you were saying how much you hated him, and now he is gone. Let's just move on."

"He's a good guy, Melissa! I should have been the one to move on and..."

"Jack Avery, I am so done with you right now. I can't believe you. I thought I'd come home and you would be in a good mood. You are one selfish pig!" Melissa briskly walked up the steps, slamming the front door behind her. Jack was left dumbfounded out in the heat of a hot summer evening.

Once again Jack found himself on the couch unable to sleep. The evening had been miserable. Melissa didn't bother to make dinner or even attempt to rectify the mood after the bad fight in the front yard. In fact, Jack hadn't seen her since the argument. She was in her room all evening. He made Olivia a simple dinner but he was too upset and confused to eat, and now he lay on the couch on the verge of tears. He wondered if he had come on too strong. She was only trying to help and make his life in Singleton a little easier.

He thought for a while about apologizing, but there were other issues about the argument that troubled him. How was Gus fired so abruptly? It was yesterday evening that Jack was telling Melissa about how overbearing Gus could be and come this morning at work Gus had been let go. Jack assumed Melissa got her father involved and he had pulled some strings and had him fired, but he wondered how this could be. How could things have been put into motion so quickly? The Averys' phone still had not been set up and she couldn't be sneaking a cell phone since the cell phone tower was still down. He wondered if they had actually been talking past one another, like maybe they were talking about two different situations and hadn't realized it. To the best of his memory, Jack ran the conversation through his mind again. He tried to make sure there was no area where she could have misunderstood him.

He didn't get far in his thoughts when he heard a crash in the kitchen. Jack arose from the couch, running over to see what had happened. He was in his undershirt but still in his dress pants. He hadn't had the opportunity to change because Melissa kept him out of his bedroom all evening.

In the kitchen he found glass shards all over the floor along with a brick. Someone had obviously thrown it through one of the front windows. This was the first sign of vandalism since the incident with the eggs earlier in the week. He walked over to the window; looking out he saw no one. He figured someone was really trying to get his attention and to let them know that they were not welcomed in this town. Was this the same teenage boy he saw earlier in the week or could this have been Gus in retaliation? Gus seemed so harmless, but he had just lost his job of twenty-five years.

He stood staring at the glass-filled floor when the kitchen light came on. Melissa and Olivia had also been awakened by the crash. Both appeared stunned by what they saw. Melissa was the first to speak up, "Jack, what's going on?"

"I don't know. I just heard the crash and ran over."

"Did you see anyone?"

"No, I looked out the window, but there's no one around. What is going on?" Jack said frustrated. He took a seat at one of the dining room chairs, burying his face into his hands, "Melissa, you always said things like this didn't happen in Singleton. Who is doing this?"

Melissa stood there shaking her head, completely confused by the whole ordeal.

Jack couldn't take it anymore, "All right, that's it, tomorrow we are packing this place up and we are leaving Singleton!"

Chapter 12

Jack couldn't sleep. He looked over at the clock which read 3:00 a.m. Melissa had softened her tone after the brick was thrown through the window. Jack couldn't tell if she was scared or just confused, but she seemed to have no problem allowing him back into the bedroom. He wondered why all this was happening. Why were they being targeted like this? Melissa seemed to have the same questions as well.

He kept thinking about all the things that needed to be done before they left. He couldn't believe they were leaving so soon. It excited him. His house in Denver had not yet sold, so it would be easy to move right back into their home. As soon as they got outside of town, Jack would call his realtor and tell him to take the house off the market. He wondered if Alex would want them to take the furniture he bought for them or if they should just leave it. Either way he didn't care, he just wanted to get out of there.

He eventually fell asleep around four and awoke a little after six. Even with so little sleep, he felt well rested. His adrenaline immediately kicked into gear. He was ready to pack their belongings and head home.

As he climbed out of bed Melissa softly spoke up, "Jack, don't you think you are acting a little too rash? Why don't you just come back to bed and get some more sleep? Everyone in town knows about this incident and hopefully the stupid kid who is doing this will be caught soon."

"Melissa, it's more than just the vandalism. Our relationship has been drastically up and down since we got here, my job seems so useless and unfulfilling, and Olivia hasn't been herself either. It seems like things are just going to get worse. I think we need to get out of here as soon as possible."

"Ok, if you say so, Jack," Melissa said, turning over on her side, facing away from Jack. She knew there was no point in arguing with her husband. He had made up his mind.

Jack headed for the bathroom and got ready for the day. He assumed Olivia heard him last night and would understand his impulsive decision to head back to Denver. He thought he would let her sleep in. Jack showered as quickly as he could. He was ready to head out of town immediately to the nearest U-Haul dealer.

He finished getting dressed and quickly left his bedroom. Quietly he shut his bedroom door, not wanting to disturb Melissa. She was apparently in somewhat of a good mood this morning and he didn't want to break any rapport he had with her.

Walking past Olivia's room, he saw her light on. Could she already be awake? It wasn't even seven o'clock. Did she fall asleep with the light on? He decided to knock, "Olivia, are you awake?" Jack said quietly.

She answered back immediately, "Yep, I'm fine, Dad."

He was puzzled, "Why are you up so early, Sweetie?"

"I don't know. I was just thinking about some things."

"Ok, well, is there anything I can help you with?"

"No, I'll be fine. I just need to organize some stuff in here before I pack."

Jack wanted to pry more, but he was determined to pack up and leave as soon as possible. "Ok, well, let me know if you need anything. I'm going to head out of town to pick up a trailer. I hope it will only take an hour or so."

"All right, sounds good, Dad," Olivia said half-heartedly. Jack was very puzzled by her behavior. What was she doing this morning? Was she just so anxious to leave that, like her father, she couldn't sleep? Jack had always felt there were *mysteries* surrounding Olivia and her life, but this week in Singleton seemed to exaggerate them even more.

He headed outside. The sun was just rising and the air felt strangely cool. Just a bit of rain had fallen in Singleton last night. As he approached his car, he couldn't believe it had only been a week since they arrived. It seemed like so much had happened since they left Denver.

He got into his car and took out his keys. He put them into the ignition and turned...he heard nothing. He tried again...same result. He pulled them out and put them back in...same result. The car was dead. Jack couldn't believe it. He sat in silence, staring at the steering wheel, wondering what was going on. It was like the town was keeping him here, not wanting him to leave. He felt like the town had come alive and was holding onto him, refusing to let go and torturing him.

After a couple of minutes of silence, he resolved that this would not hold him back. He *was* going to leave this town. He got out of his car and looked under the hood. Everything looked fine, but then again Jack knew next to nothing about how the engine of a car worked. Nothing seemed out of place. He shut the hood and looked underneath the car. Once again, nothing looked out of place. Frustrated out of his mind, Jack took a seat on the ground with his back resting against the front bumper.

He was at a total loss about what to do. Part of him felt like he would never leave this town. He tried to keep telling himself that this was just a small bump in the road. He would get this fixed and they would be on their way in a few days, no big deal. He wanted to leave Singleton so badly that he even thought about selling his car on the spot and buying a new one outright. Sure, it was an old station wagon, but then again he thought he could still get a couple thousand out of it.

Jack was lost deep in thought when a sound snapped him out of it. It was coming from the backyard. It sounded like someone was back there. He walked around the side of his house, slowly peeking around each corner. He was sure he heard something moving. Looking around in the backyard, he saw nothing. The yard seemed to be in good shape, the fence looked fine, nothing broken. He checked the windows and thankfully there were no signs of eggs or broken glass, but *wait*...there was something out of place. Olivia's window was open. It could only be opened from the inside. He called out to his daughter, "Olivia...Olivia!"

Walking over to the window, he noticed the bushes were moving slightly. He took a closer look and sure enough there she was, Olivia, hiding in the bushes, hoping her father would not find her. She looked just a little scared.

Jack spoke to her, "Olivia, what are you doing?"

"I just wanted to go outside and get some fresh air," she said nervously.

"But why the window?"

"Dad, shhh, she will hear you," Olivia said quietly. Jack felt a wide range of emotions. He was frustrated by the situation with the car. He was confused by Olivia's need to sneak out of her bedroom window. And he was saddened by the fact that Olivia was doing so much sneaking around her mother. Was she just hiding because Melissa would not approve of her playing outside so early in the morning? Melissa did not approve of a lot of things Olivia did, but most of the time she just took the consequences of her mother's anger.

Jack, at a complete loss for words, just stood there in silence with Olivia. He was ready to give up. He had no idea what he should do next. He took a seat beside Olivia on the ground. Feeling totally dejected, Jack tried to think of his next move. What could he do to fix the car? How could he repair his relationship with Melissa? How could he figure out what was going on with Olivia? After sitting in silence with his daughter for what had to be fifteen minutes, he thought of the best thing he could do at the moment.

"Olivia!"

"Yes, Dad?" Her head was buried between her knees, not wanting to face her father.

"Let's go fishing."

♋

Jack remembered from looking at a map back in Denver, Font Lake was just to the east of his house. Since they didn't have internet access in Singleton, Jack had to go off his memory. It was about a two mile walk to the lake, which wasn't much compared to all the hiking he and Olivia had done on their various trips. They were getting close to the lake, but they were now traveling through a dense, wooded area and were following a very faint path.

"This reminds me of the time we flew out east and did that trip through the Smokey Mountains," Jack said, ducking under some limbs that were hanging low. He held them up for Olivia to pass under. He continued, "We need to do another trip like that sometime soon. It's nice being out in the dense woods after spending so much time in the Rocky Mountains. Olivia, what do you think about traveling to the Northeast, say New Hampshire, and possibly spending a whole week out in the woods? Maybe next summer?"

"Sure, that sounds nice," Olivia said very unenthusiastically. Her mind was definitely somewhere else. So far she hadn't said much on this walk.

"Or we could try North Georgia? I hear there are some beautiful trails down there."

"That's fine, wherever," Olivia said, not even bothering to look up at her father.

Jack couldn't take Olivia's attitude. He decided to be up front and honest and just try to hit these issues head on. "Olivia, please tell me what's going on! Why do you keep pushing Mom away? I know she can be a little overbearing at times, but it might soften her mood a little if she sees you wanting to spend time with her. You know, maybe just give her a chance."

This did not get a reaction from Olivia. She just kept on walking as if Jack had said nothing. He was getting angry at her resistance and decided to just lay it all out on the table. "You know, Olivia, you should be grounded for a month for hiding so much from your mother. Why not just tell her about the incident in the woods, or just tell her you want to go outside instead of sneaking out the window? Why are you hiding so much from her?"

"For the same reason you are, Dad," Olivia said calmly.

Jack stopped in his tracks. He couldn't believe what he just heard. "Olivia, what do you mean by that? I'm not hiding anything," Jack shot back.

"Dad, have you told Mom about me exploring the woods?"

"Well, no, I guess I haven't."

She kept going, "Or what about the boy you saw on our first night, the one who egged the house? Does Mom know about him too?"

She had a point. Jack was deliberately keeping these things from her. He wondered how Olivia knew about the boy. "Olivia, how do you know about him? Did you see him too? Out the window?"

"No, I didn't, but I did talk to him a couple of days later when you were at work."

"What? Olivia, you actually talked to the guy? Did you tell him to stop? Why is he doing all this? Why is he vandalizing our house?"

"Dad, why don't you ask him yourself? I'm sure he will come around again if you give him enough time."

"Olivia, I don't want you talking to him again. What if he's dangerous?"

Olivia smiled just slightly, looking at the ground to watch her steps, "Oh, trust me, Dad, he's not dangerous. He's just a kid. You ought to just try to talk to him."

"Olivia, he vandalized our house! This is crazy. I don't know why you are keeping all this from me. Listen, I just felt like I couldn't tell Mom I saw him because...well, you know how you mom is, she would just be extremely angry at this kid, and I wanted to talk with him first. In a way, I was protecting him from her."

Olivia stood silent for a moment before she shot back, "Well, Dad, maybe that's the reason I'm keeping these things from Mom."

"What? What do you mean?"

"For protection!"

"Protection for this kid? Olivia, I don't understand."

"No Dad, not for him, but for us!"

"Why do we need protection from Mom?"

"I don't think she likes us, Dad, or wants us around. I think she's planning something with Grandpa. I see them whispering a lot like they are hiding things from us."

This hit Jack like a ton of bricks. Half of him thought this whole conversation was absurd or crazy, but the other half thought there might be a point to what Olivia was saying. He very much didn't want to believe it. He was still holding out hope that there was some giant misunderstanding in Olivia's mind and as soon as they got back to Denver, everything was going to be all right.

"Listen, Olivia, this is crazy! You know your mom loves you and would never do anything to harm us," Jack said, trying to sound convincing, "It's just that things have been stressful lately, and I think everything will get better once we get back to Denver. Once we are back we can go from there and..."

Jack was suddenly taken off guard by what he saw in the distance. It was about thirty feet away. The woods were thick but he could see through them enough to see something. He picked up his pace, weaving through tree branches and brush. Olivia followed closely behind, wondering what was going on.

He made his way down the faint path to a fence, a chain-link fence about six feet in height. There was barbed wire at the top. In the middle of the fence where the path had led them, there was a large sign, which read in bold letters, "DO NOT ENTER UNDER ANY CIRCUMSTANCE". Jack wondered, *What could be inside? Why the strict warning?*

"Dad, what is this? Shouldn't the lake be inside the fence?" Olivia said.

"Yes, it should be just inside." Jack put his hand on the fence and peeked through it, trying to figure out how much further the lake was. He wondered if they would be able to see anything more if they kept walking along the outside of the fence.

"Why do you think they are trying to keep people out?" Olivia asked.

"I'm not sure, Sweetie, maybe the lake is contaminated somehow, or maybe there is some type of endangered fish or something like that." Jack walked a little to his right and looked through the woods to see if there was an end to this fence. It looked like it had been there for a while; parts of it were rusted. Upon running his fingers over it, he found it was a little thicker than an average chain-link fence. It was too thick to be cut with a pair of pliers. It was quite obvious that the person who designed it didn't want anyone entering this area under any circumstance.

While inspecting the fence, a key question hit Jack: Why did he not know about this area, especially because it was so close to their house? Surely Melissa would have said something about this. In all their discussions about Singleton, not once did Melissa say anything about a restricted lake. She knew that he and Olivia would probably go fishing in the area, so why didn't she warn him about it?

All of these questions swirled in Jack's mind. He wondered what he should do with Olivia. He didn't want to disappoint her, but yet she seemed to be just as inquisitive about the situation as he. Hopefully she would understand. "Olivia, I'm thinking we have to turn around. I'm not sure what is going on here."

"I understand," she replied.

As they left the fence, Jack decided that this was one mystery that was not going to be left unsolved. For some reason, he felt that inside that fence lay the answers to many of the questions he had about this town. When he got home, he would confront Melissa head-on about this area.

Chapter 13

Melissa was startled when Jack and Olivia came through the door with their fishing gear. She had no idea they had tried to go fishing. It was barely past eight and they hadn't communicated since early that morning.

"Jack, what are you doing? I thought you'd be packing the car right now," Melissa said.

"Olivia, do you mind going to your room? Mom and I need to talk." Jack said, ignoring Melissa's questions. Olivia headed to her room without objecting.

"Jack, what's going on? Where did you go fishing?"

"Melissa, what is going on with Font Lake?"

"What are you talking about, Jack?"

"Font Lake! Listen, the car wouldn't start this morning and Olivia was awake so instead of me trying to take it somewhere early on a Saturday morning, we just decided to go fishing before we did more packing, and…"

She interrupted him, "What, the car won't start? What's wrong with it?"

"How should I know?" Jack said, getting close to shouting. "We don't have phone service. How am I supposed to contact someone to come look at it?"

"Calm down, Jack! You're acting like some kid having a tantrum. We will get the car fixed soon enough. My father will come around and help us."

Just the mention of Melissa's father made Jack angrier, but he wasn't going to be thrown off course from his initial question. "Ok, listen to me! What is going on with Font Lake?" Jack said emphatically.

"Jack, I don't know what you are talking about!"

"Olivia and I tried to walk there this morning, but in the woods we came to this large fence that said..."

"Jack! I told you both back in Denver to stay out of those woods! Why were you messing around over there? I can't believe you! You don't listen to anything I say!"

Jack was determined not to be intimidated this time. He walked over to the kitchen table and rested both hands on it. Melissa's purse was nearby. He was trying to calm himself. "Melissa, what is going on with Font Lake?"

"Jack, you are being such a spoiled brat and..."

He would not let her finish, "Melissa, I want to know about the lake. Tell me about it now!"

"Jack, you're crazy! There's no lake anywhere around here. I told you to stay out of the woods. I can't believe I married such a lousy husband who doesn't even listen to his wife."

Jack couldn't take it anymore. In a fit of rage he picked up her purse and threw it against the wall. The purse looked like it exploded. It fell to the ground, spilling out all of its contents.

Melissa, putting her hands on her head, shouted, "Jack, what are you doing? How dare you touch my purse! You could have broken something, you idiot! I don't know what I ever saw in you or how I stayed with you for this long. You are an incredibly selfish pig!"

Jack didn't hear a word she said. He was focused on what fell out of the purse. Walking over to it, he reached through a pile of cosmetics to pick up the curious object he saw. Melissa objected, "Jack, what are you doing? That's not yours!"

Picking it up, he showed it to Melissa, "What's this?" He said matter-of-factly. Jack wasn't necessarily waiting for an answer from Melissa. He knew what it was he was holding. It was a phone, but not a cell phone. It was quite a bit larger than a modern cell phone and had a large antenna protruding out of the top. It was a satellite phone.

"Jack, that's none of your business! That's for me!"

"How long have you had this?"

Melissa rushed over to where her purse lay, ignoring his question. She ripped the phone out of Jack's hands, quickly gathering her things and stuffing them back into her purse.

"Why were you hiding this from me? What is going on?" Jack shouted.

Standing up, Melissa put her purse over her shoulder and struck Jack hard across the face, slapping him hard with her bare hand. Wanting so badly to retaliate verbally, Jack restrained his anger. Melissa walked briskly over to the front door and walked out. Jack had no idea where she was going. Feeling exhausted from the fight, he fell to the ground on both knees and began to cry. He started to second guess everything he had just said.

How could this have happened? Did he let his anger get the best of him? He thought he should have just waited to bring up all these questions with Melissa when he got back to Denver. He wished he had just kept appeasing her a little while longer until they arrived back home. He didn't know what to do and he had so many questions. Why was Melissa hiding this phone from him? Why didn't she tell him about it? Had he let their marriage get so bad that she felt she couldn't tell him she possessed a satellite phone? Once again, Jack was at a loss and didn't know what to do.

☾

It was getting late in the afternoon. Jack sat on the couch with the curtains open. It had been storming hard all day. He basically hadn't moved much since Melissa left. Olivia had occasionally come out of her room to comfort her father. She had heard most of the argument since both of her parents' voices had been raised. It didn't seem to bother her as much as Jack might have thought. She seemed calm, steady, and ready for whatever would happen next. Jack admired her for this.

As he thought back to the argument, there was something Melissa had said that Jack couldn't shake. He kept thinking about it, trying to recall the exact words she used. "There is no lake nearby!" Is that what she said? How could she not know about Font Lake? Sure, it wasn't very big, but for a girl who had lived in Singleton her whole life, surely she would have known about it. Jack remembered looking at the map before he left Denver, and if his memory served him correctly, he couldn't have been that far off. He was determined to explore the area more as soon as the rain let up a little. They had received so much rain over the past three hours that Jack figured there might be a flash flood warning issued soon.

He thought he would try to lie down and get some rest since he had been up early in order to drive out of town to pick up a trailer. He headed for his bedroom. Thinking that the rain was not going to let up anytime soon, he thought he would crawl into bed for an extended nap. He knew it would be difficult to relax with the situation with Melissa at hand, but yet he was also so exhausted from all of it that he thought he could sleep. Sitting down on the edge of his bed, Jack pulled up the blinds so he could keep an eye on the rain as he fell asleep. He had always thought there was something soothing about the hard rain coming down, hitting his windows.

He took off his outer shirt and threw it on the ground. He was ready to pull off his undershirt when he noticed something out of the corner of his eye, something in the backyard. He got up and walked closer to the window to get a closer look. The rain coming down in sheets made it hard to see. In the corner of the backyard along the fence, he saw a figure hiding in the bushes in rain gear. The figure moved his hands as if he was preparing something. Jack watched for what seemed like five minutes when the figure emerged from the bushes and slowly approached the window. He could tell it was a boy, and not just any boy, but the same boy who had been vandalizing the house. Jack had seen him twice and knew it was him.

As soon as Jack realized this kid was going to take another crack with an egg, he bolted for the back door. Not only was he going to stop this kid, but he wanted answers. He was determined not to let him get away this time. He opened up the back door and launched himself out, shouting, "Hey, you, stop right there!"

With that the boy dropped the eggs and ran for the back fence. Jack ran after him, thinking he was trapped. The boy approached the fence and with one great leap he grabbed the top of the wooden fence and threw himself over. Jack was not going to let this stop him. He meticulously climbed over the fence, hoping the boy hadn't gotten too far. Reaching the top, he saw the boy about thirty yards away looking back at him. Coming down the backside of the fence, Jack slipped on the wet surface and fell to the ground, landing face first in a mud puddle. His white undershirt was now covered in mud. The fall knocked the wind out of him. He did not move.

The boy came a few steps closer, thinking Jack injured himself on the fall. When he got within a few feet, Jack seized the opportunity and lunged forward, tackling him. The boy quickly rolled Jack off himself and broke free. The teenage boy quickly got back on his feet and took off running again. Jack followed close behind.

They ran close to a mile and a half through a few back yards, over fences, and through streets. Jack was losing ground on the kid but still had him in sight. The rain was coming down so strong that it was even hard to run through it. The wind was also slowing him down, but Jack wasn't going to let anything stop him. He directed all of his emotions and energy toward this chase.

♋

Olivia was in her bedroom when she saw her father run after the boy. She was not afraid. She knew things were finally going to be put in motion. What would happen to her father? Would he be ok? Was there anything she could do to help him believe? She knew that after today her life would be forever changed. The past three years had been a joy living with the Avery family, particularly with her father.

She thought back to the nuns at St. Thomas' Children's Home. She wondered if she would ever see them again. They had poured out their love on her and made sure she felt at home. The day she was adopted was bittersweet for them. They were happy for her having a family, but also sad, knowing that her sweet face would no longer be part of their lives.

Olivia sat down on the side of bed, wondering how long it would be before her father returned. She wanted to wait for him, but she didn't want to be home alone if her mother returned. In the back of her mind Olivia hoped she would never see her again. She felt bad for thinking this, but she knew her mother was not concerned for the well being of her or her father.

She knelt beside her bed. She learned how to pray while living with the nuns. "Dear God, I pray that you would help me now. I need your strength to face these hard things. Please be with Daddy. Help him not to get hurt and for him to be ok. I need you, God, for what I am about to do. I need you now. I pray these things in the name of the Father, the Son, and the Holy Ghost. Amen."

♋

They had run for nearly three miles. Jack's shoes were completely covered in mud. He had a little blood running from his elbow from the earlier fall from his fence. He was breathing heavily. His muscles ached. A part of him wanted to stop, but another part of him said to keep running. He had so many questions in his mind and he needed answers.

Jack was running out of stamina when, finally, instead of running through another backyard, the boy ran through the back door of a house. This house seemed to be a little isolated, about fifty yards away from its neighbors. It was an old house with its white paint beginning to chip away. Jack arrived about a half minute after the boy. There was a small red baseball bat lying on the grass. Jack picked it up, fearing that there might be some trouble coming.

He approached the back door, trying to see if he could spot anyone through the window on the door. He was about to knock on the door when he noticed that it wasn't fully shut. He knocked softly and it creaked open. Jack opened it a little wider. It was dark inside. He could tell by some of the décor and old furniture that the house probably belonged to an elderly woman. He decided to shout out, "Hello...Hello." No answer. "Is anyone home?" he said, pushing the door completely open.

He tried again, "Hello...I just want to talk." He began to take a few steps into the house. He continued on, "I just want to ask you a few questions." Jack noticed a few old pictures on the wall, a lot of family pictures. He walked through the kitchen. Looking out the window, he could see the rain coming down strong, along with lightning. He felt a little strange being in someone's house uninvited, but yet he felt the boy had left the door open for him.

Turning a corner, Jack approached the living room. He saw some light coming from the room. As he got closer, he realized that a large fire was burning in the fireplace. It was the only light in the house. A slight bit of movement coming from a chair caught Jack's attention. It was a rocking chair, moving ever so slightly. It was facing the fire, and from the top of it he could see that someone was rocking calmly. It was an old woman.

Jack approached her ever so carefully, when she spoke up, "Welcome, Jack Avery, I have been expecting you for a long time."

Chapter 14

Jack took a seat close to the fire. Even though he was in the house of a complete stranger, he felt at ease. Now that he was seated and resting by the fire, he realized how cold he was. He was completely soaked. He had been so caught up in the moment, chasing the teenage boy, that he hadn't realized how cold and wet he had become. He was wet down to his socks and underwear. The fire felt wonderful.

"How 'bout a cup of tea for ya?" the old woman said. She had a very pleasant voice. It reminded him of his grandmother.

"Sure, that would be great," Jack said calmly. At the moment he was still taking everything in, trying to be observant of his surroundings, seeing if he could spot anything that would give him a clue as to what was going on.

"Nick...Nick, you can come out now. I don't think Jack's worried about you any longer," the woman spoke to a hidden figure down the hallway. The boy Jack had been chasing appeared. He looked straight at Jack. He was about six feet in height, with brown hair, and he looked to be in great shape, like a wrestler or an athlete of some type. He appeared to be a little timid to show his face. Possibly he was afraid Jack was going to take another opportunity to pounce on him.

She continued, "Nick, it's ok, you have nothing to be scared of. I think Jack is beginning to realize what's happening."

Jack was stunned, "I beg your pardon, ma'am, but I have no idea what is going on. If you could enlighten me, that would be a huge help."

"Oh, Jack, why don't we talk it through over a nice cup of tea? Nick, Dear, if you wouldn't mind, please fetch us a couple of cups?"

With that, Nick walked to the kitchen with his head down, not wanting to face Jack as he walked by. The old woman kept rocking in her chair very peacefully and at ease. She had to be in her upper eighties. She looked very frail, not much meat on her bones. Her hair was nicely kept. What Jack couldn't get over was her confidence. Not so much in the things she said, but in her look. She wasn't afraid of Jack. She looked squarely at him when speaking. Though she was frail, she was full of strength.

She continued, "Now, Jack, why don't you go ahead and ask me the one question that is on your mind, the one you have thought about for a long time."

"Like why has Nick here been egging and vandalizing our house?" Jack said, pointing over to the kitchen.

"NO, Jack!" She shot back, "Don't be so naïve. We were only trying to get your attention. Don't blame this on Nick. He's a pretty good kid. I merely needed someone to do my dirty work. As you can see, I'm past the point of doing things on my own."

"Who are you?"

"Jack, must we do all these preliminary greetings. If you haven't figured it out by now, I'm Betty Louise."

"Oh! I've heard about you," Jack said, somewhat embarrassed that those words came from his mouth. All he ever heard about her was negative.

"Yes, you probably heard I was the woman who has gone mad. I'm sure you heard a few years back that I struck my windows with a baseball bat in an angry rage."

The tea arrived. Nick gave a cup to each of them before retreating to the dining room. Jack took a sip, hoping to warm himself. The storm brought more flashes of lightning. With each strike, the room lit up and Jack could see the scores of pictures on the wall and in frames. Most were in black and white. He could tell this woman knew much of her heritage.

Jack continued, "What happened? Why the bat? Is it true?"

"Jack, must we do this? Yes, it's true. Well, partially true. I was severely angry with my son and the men he had with him. I couldn't take it anymore and lashed out. As you can see I keep a lot of nostalgia around the house. That old bat you are holding was nearby. I picked it up and threw it at him. Silly me, I missed him and completely smashed one of my windows." she said calmly.

All of a sudden, Jack felt afraid, like he was sitting in the presence of a mad old woman, who was ready to lash out at any moment. He couldn't see how this woman could ever be that angry, and especially with her own son. He thought about leaving, but realized that Nick might be acting as her bodyguard. Though he was probably only seventeen or eighteen, he had already proven he was in a lot better shape than Jack. He would probably just tackle Jack if he tried to leave. Betty had worked so hard to get Jack here, so most likely she was not about to let him just walk out. He decided to stay put and sip his tea. He did have a lot of questions for Betty, but it was apparent she only wanted to answer one.

"What is going on in Singleton? What is this town doing?" Jack asked, hoping she would bite on his questions.

"Jack, be honest with yourself, this is not the foremost question in your mind. I don't know why you aren't asking it. Perhaps we should jog your memory just a bit." She placed her tea on the table beside her. The thunder and lightning were going strong, but no one seemed to notice at the moment. She continued, "Nick, Dear, would you please bring in the item I told you about? It's in the back room."

Nick stood up and walked to one of the back bedrooms. In that moment neither Jack nor Betty said a word. She was relaxed. Her head was resting gently against the back of her chair as she rocked ever so slightly. She was in no hurry. It seemed to Jack that her top priority was making sure he understood what was happening.

Jack lifted his cup to his mouth. Nick stood in the hallway entrance holding the item in his hands. Jack almost spit out his tea. He quickly swallowed, "Where did you get that? Why did you take it? Give it to me!"

"Hold on, Jack," Betty interrupted, "We didn't take anything...well, not from you at least. Alex's moving crew, of course, got it from Olivia's bag. I then had my great-nephew, Nick here, break into Alex's house and steal it from him. We didn't want him to discover what was inside." Nick brought it over to her and set it in her lap. Jack sat there staring at what she was now holding. It was Olivia's box. He would know that cream colored box anywhere. It looked the same as the last time Jack saw it. Obviously Betty and Nick had taken great care of it.

She looked straight at him, "Now, Jack, would you like to ask me what you are wondering? Please ask me your question. The one you've had for a long time."

He sat silent for a few seconds, staring at the box. He knew exactly what she was referring to. How did Betty know that this question had been on his mind for such a long time? He thought about it in some form every day. He couldn't believe he was about to ask it. "Who is she...Olivia?"

Betty smiled, "That's more like it, Jack." She opened the box and held it out for Jack to look inside. He saw all her normal items she kept in the box: a few rosary beads, some dollar bills, a couple of pictures, nothing out of the ordinary.

He wondered if he was supposed to find some meaning in the items.

"Betty, I don't get it. How is this supposed to tell me who she is? This is just her old stuff she has kept for a while. I don't know what you want me to see. There's nothing unusual about this stuff."

"Jack, perhaps you need to look more carefully, for things aren't always as they seem." With that Betty showed him the lid, "Look carefully." He inspected it carefully and nothing seemed out of place. Grabbing it and flipping it over, he inspected the underside. Jack noticed that an additional piece of cardboard had been placed on the bottom. He removed it gently so as not to rip or tear anything. The box was very frail and he wanted to return it to Olivia in good condition. Pulling the piece out, he found a few sheets of folded-up notebook paper. It looked to be about six total.

"What are they?" he asked.

"See for yourself," Betty responded.

He unfolded one and could tell right away that it was a letter. It was not Olivia's handwriting. Reading the date at the top, Jack realized it was written a couple of years before her adoption. These were letters sent to Olivia while she was in the children's home. It read:

Dearest Olivia,

I hope all is well and you are enjoying life. Remember to always be a good girl and listen to the nuns. I know they may seem like old hags at times, but they are looking out for your safety and I'm sure they love you very much. Remember to stay close to them and do as you're told.

I know by this time you are getting older and are probably wondering why I left you. I imagine these questions will always be on your mind. I hope these letters can be a source of comfort and assurance that I love you and never wanted to leave you, but know that I had to for your own safety. Remember that people are chasing you and they will never stop until they have you. You must be prepared, always prepared to run. Though you cannot defeat them, you can hide from them. Keep this letter always, read it when you are older, cling to it and remember what I've said.

Though I will never watch you grow up, be assured that I will always love you and think of you. My biggest comfort in life is knowing you are safe and sound.

Love always,

Dad

Jack couldn't believe what he had just read. Many different thoughts passed through his mind. He opened the other letters and read through them briefly. They all said basically the same thing. They reassured Olivia that she was loved and needed to be ready to run. Obviously they were from her biological father. What was he warning her about? Why did she need to keep running? This all seemed crazy to

Jack. Though things in Singleton had not been normal, he didn't want to believe any of this. This woman seemed to be, indeed, certifiably crazy; why should he believe anything she said? He became angry.

Standing up, he threw the letters to the ground. "Listen, I've got to get home. This is crazy. Olivia needs me right now with her mother being gone. I don't have time for all these games. How did you say you got this box anyway?"

Betty sat patiently, not being stirred by Jack's temper or his disbelief, "Jack, as I said, I stole it...well, actually I didn't steal it, but Nick here did."

"Answer me honestly! Did you get it out of Olivia's bag?" Jack said, trying to make sure she wasn't lying.

"No, don't be foolish, Nick stole it from my son."

"Your son!"

"Yes, my son. You see, my real name is Elizabeth Louise Wellington. Alex is my son."

"What?!" Jack said, shocked.

"Yes, he knew Olivia's biological father was writing her and he wanted to know how much she knew," Betty said calmly.

Was this true? Jack was in a quandary. He didn't know whether to believe all this or not. This woman had a reputation for being crazy. Maybe she just wanted some fame or prestige for being the mother of Alex Wellington and she would be glad to tell it to whoever would believe it. He wanted to leave as fast as possible. "Listen, I appreciate the tea and the hot fire, but I'm going home. We're leaving

Singleton as soon as we can. I'll do you two a favor and not press charges, if you leave me and my family alone."

Her voice rose slightly, "I feared this would happen. Jack, you are so stubborn and are denying the obvious. Think about everything you know about Olivia. Doesn't it ring true that there is more to her than what you know? Open your eyes, Jack!"

Jack turned to look at the fire, struggling with what to do. Should he listen to this woman who claimed to be his wife's grandmother? Or should he just walk out and leave all this behind? Betty could tell he needed more. He needed to see more in order to believe.

"Jack, may I show you one more thing?"

He turned around, speechless, staring at Betty. Seeing her look of sincerity, he whispered under his breath, "Sure."

"Listen, to me! I want you to follow Nick. He is going to take you somewhere where your questions will be answered. After that, you can go on your way...sound fair?"

What would it hurt? Jack thought if he could see a little more he could possibly tell if what Betty was telling him was true or false. "Ok," he said quietly.

She looked over at Nick, "Very good! Nick, you know what to do. Please, if you would, go out the back. There may be people watching."

Nick nodded, "Let's go, Jack, follow me."

Jack began to follow Nick when he realized there may a possibility he may never see Betty again. There was one more question he had for her. Something she said earlier made him very curious. He stopped and turned to her, "Betty, one more question before I go."

"If you must," she answered.

"Why were you angry with your son? What did he do that made you lash out in anger?"

"Jack, Dear, I'm surprised you haven't figured it out yet. He vowed to never stop chasing her."

"Who is he chasing?"

"The girl you now call Olivia."

Chapter 15

Nick led Jack through the basement, out a cellar door. From there they traveled through the outer rim of town, mostly in the woods. They were trying to be discreet, not wanting anyone to see them. The rain was still coming down hard. Thankfully Nick had supplied Jack with a rain jacket before they left the house. It was approaching eight o'clock and the heavy dark clouds made the evening darker than usual for that time in August. Jack hadn't asked Nick any questions as the rain made it difficult to chat, and, besides, Nick was walking at such a brisk pace that Jack felt he was probably not in the mood for questions.

They approached the downtown area of Singleton. The rain started to let up just a bit. "Get down!" Nick said as he ducked behind a bush. Jack followed suit. A car flew past them on the road. Another one followed. Wherever they were going, Nick did not want to be seen.

As they crouched behind the bushes, Jack spoke up, "Where are you taking me?"

"To the library," Nick said, peeking through the bushes. "There is something there that will answer most of your questions."

Jack thought this was odd. Most libraries were closed on Saturday evenings, and besides, why did they need to sneak over to the library?

"Let's go," Nick said, standing up. He led off quickly, trying to stay obscure, ducking behind trees and bushes when necessary. Jack was ready to give this up and go home, when they made it to the library. They went around back. There was a small storage door hidden from the direct view of the road. Nick grabbed a lock pick from his pocket and went to work on the lock.

"What are you doing?" Jack yelled. The library was obviously closed.

"Shh, you're going to get us caught," Nick said sternly.

"I didn't know we were going to break into the library; this is crazy! I'm going home!"

At that moment, the door swung open slowly. Nick, paying no attention to Jack, stepped inside. "Come on!" he said, waving Jack into the dark building. Jack stood there for a moment, weighing his options. Could he really go home from here? He figured that if he left he would always wonder what Nick was going to show him inside the library. His curiosity overcame the consequences he would endure if caught. He entered the library.

Nick was far ahead of him, already to the top of the nearby stairwell. Everything was dark. The exit signs gave just enough light for Jack to see where he was going. He followed Nick up the flight of stairs. At the top of the stairs they entered a door into the main floor of the library. Jack had never been to Singleton's library, but it looked normal at first glance. It was a relatively small library with the usual categories of books. He could see signs for fiction, biographies, history, language, etc. Nothing looked out of place.

Nick made his way over to the front desk counter near the main entrance. He ducked behind the counter in order to conceal himself from the nearby front window. Jack caught up to him and ducked beside him. Nick was exploring the contents of one of the cabinets of the desk.

Jack wanted answers, "Nick, what are you doing here? Is this what you wanted to show me?"

"No, I'm just looking for the key," Nick said. He was focused and didn't even bother to look at Jack. He was clearing out the miscellaneous supplies and books in the cabinet in order to get to the bottom. Once it was clear, he pulled up a small section of the cabinet's floor. Jack heard something crack. Reaching through the hole he created, Nick pulled out a small tin lunch box. It looked to be from the 1970s. Opening it up, he pulled out a small envelope. He quickly opened it up and dumped a small key into his hand.

"What is going on?" Jack asked, dumbfounded, "How did you know that was there?"

"It took months of questions and inquiries to figure out its location," Nick whispered, "Jack, if you haven't realized by now, we are part of a resistance."

"A resistance against what?"

"Shh, Jack, keep your voice down," Nick said calmly. More questions swirled in Jack's mind. It was not the proper time to delve into all these things with Nick. They were so close to the front entrance, Jack was mainly concerned with not getting caught.

Nick quickly put the contents of the cabinet back into place. He looked around one more time before getting up and continuing onto another section of the library. Jack followed close behind.

Nick led him to a section of the library entitled Archives. It was mostly filled with old journals and statistical data for the city. These were books that would rarely be used. There was dust everywhere. They came to a small bookcase in the back corner of the library—more archive books. Jack wondered what Nick wanted to show him at this book case.

"Grab that side," Nick whispered. He was already on one side, ready to move it. Jack felt he was past the point of asking questions. He grabbed the other side and they pulled the case a few feet from the wall. A couple of books fell off as they moved it. Jack reached down to pick them up.

"Quick, there's no time," Nick whispered. Jack saw that the bookcase was hiding a small wooden door. It had to be no more than three feet in height. There was a small key hole in the door. Nick produced the key from his pocket and unlocked the door. Swinging it open, Jack could see the door hid a descending stairwell. At this moment, Jack realized that Betty's conspiracy theory was true. In honesty, he knew it was true from the start of their conversation. He just didn't want to believe it.

Nick pulled a small flashlight from his pocket to light the way. Jack followed close behind. They had descended about ten steps when they came to the bottom. The area looked to be an unfinished cellar. It was cold and dark. Jack could hear a slight dripping in the room. The only light was Nick's small flashlight. The area appeared to be empty, but as Nick shined the flashlight around the room he stopped on a small bookcase against the wall. There had to be no more than twenty books on the shelf, and over half of them were not books at all, but rather three-ring binders.

Jack stood for a moment taking in the atmosphere. Why were these books being hidden? He walked over to the bookcase and read the labels on the side binders. Various titles were written on the labels; most seemed to be quite random topics: *Migration to the Midwest, Early Mesopotamian Religious Practices, History of Singleton,* etc. One definitely caught his eye, *Wellington Family Lineage.* Nick lent Jack his flashlight. He picked the book up and flipped through the pages. He saw countless charts of family trees, some even dating back to the second or third century. There were a few pictures in the latter pages of the book. He knew that the Wellingtons had a long family history, but nothing this extensive. The book was interesting but he didn't think this was what Nick was trying to show him.

"Where should I look?" he asked.

"I would probably start with this one," Nick said. He reached over to the shelf and grabbed a book entitled *Singletons*. This was a printed book. It was old, possibly dating back to the sixties. Jack dusted it off. The binding creaked as he opened it. What he read was quite astounding. He read about the people of Singleton and who they were, what they believed, and how they now lived. He read various places in the book for about an hour. Nick was patient, standing by the stairwell, nervously listening to see if anyone was coming.

Jack decided to do more reading in the section of the book concerning beliefs and religious practices. There was much that Jack did not understand. Nick walked over to see what he was reading. He peeked over Jack's shoulder.

"Jack, read this section carefully," Nick said.

"I have. It is all very odd and strange stuff," he responded.

"Re-read it carefully," Nick said, looking straight at Jack.

He flipped back a few pages and re-read the section of the book entitled *Beliefs & Religious Practices*. After a couple of minutes Jack found what he was looking for. He realized what he was reading. He stood up, shocked at what he had just read. He couldn't believe it. He re-read the section a couple of times in disbelief. He knew what Olivia had seen in the woods.

♋

Melissa met with her father in his large house. After the fight with Jack, she called her father who picked her up a few blocks from their house. She was a little nervous about meeting with him since things had not gone as planned. Events were not supposed to be set in motion until a week later. They were sitting comfortably in Alex's elegant living room by a roaring fire. They discussed their next move.

"Let's call a town meeting and get things moving," Melissa said, "I'm ready for him to be put away. You made me marry and live with him long enough. I'm ready for him to suffer. Let's deal with him now!"

Alex was comfortable. He was not in a hurry or flustered by his daughter's attitude. He was patient in explaining the situation to her. "Listen, you did well, we are so close. Please be patient, Melissa. You remember what happened nearly fifty years ago. If you recall, that is how The Resistance started. The people must be pruned. They need to be reminded of our history. They need to be made to believe."

"Listen, Father, we don't have time. You don't know Olivia like I know her. She is probably getting suspicious by now. Jack is too stupid to see what is happening, but I imagine she is starting to understand. We need to act now!"

Alex sat back in his chair. He was relaxed. The ceremony was not until the middle of September and he wondered if he could smooth things over and keep Jack in Singleton for another few weeks until it occurred. He didn't fear Jack leaving abruptly. Alex had made sure that the Avery's car had been rendered inoperable.

Melissa continued, "Father, The Resistance has already struck. We know they are working, trying to stop us. If they reach Jack, all is lost. We haven't even located her box yet. What if that is shown to Jack? You are not..."

He interrupted his daughter, "Melissa, you need to calm down. I'm not sure where the box is, but everything is fine. My mother no longer has any allies. We have been watching her home for a long time. We are still in a good position. We have nothing to worry about!"

"What about Henry? Have you heard from him lately?"

"No, I haven't, but he would have alerted me if anything had taken place. No one suspects that he is actively helping us. Not even the members of The Resistance would know about him. Most people in town just see him as some lazy farmer on the edge of town." Alex spoke so softly. He was not panicked.

The phone rang. Alex looked over to his daughter, "Would you be so kind as to answer that? Your father is getting old."

Melissa walked to the kitchen and answered the phone. Alex received few phone calls; the people of Singleton were intimidated by him. Only when something was of utmost importance did they call him. He looked into the fire, at peace in his home. He truly believed no one could stop him. The power he possessed over people was almost supernatural. People feared him and could be made to do whatever he wanted. This thought relaxed him, put him at ease.

He could hear Melissa talking on the phone. She sounded like something was wrong, but then again Melissa had been overly dramatic the last few days. She hung up the phone and ran back into the room. She was clearly worried.

"That was Stewart! He said he just got a report from someone in town that Jack left the house over an hour ago and was seen running through a neighborhood."

"Do they know where he went?" Alex asked.

"No!" She responded.

Alex was still very calm, "All right, Melissa, let's quickly call a town meeting. We must deal with this right away."

♋

Jack and Nick left the library. They tried to put everything back exactly as they found it. It was dark outside and still raining. Jack now believed everything. It all made sense. He believed everything Betty had told him about Olivia and Singleton. He realized that Betty and Nick were part of a resistance against Singleton and what it believed. They were working to stop certain events from taking place.

Jack was now in a hurry. He knew he had to find his daughter before it was too late. She could be in grave danger. They snuck out of town the same way they came in, ducking behind the same bushes and running through the woods.

They arrived back at Betty's house and entered through the back door. She was still sitting by the fire. Upon entering the living room, she spoke to him, "Well, Jack, are you still considering pressing charges?"

Jack ignored her question. He became anxious, wondering what his next move should be. He questioned Betty, "What should I do now? Will they come after you?"

"Jack, my boy, don't worry about me. Alex and the people of Singleton have been watching me for years. According to the laws of Singleton, the matriarchal leader is to be held in high regards. They won't do anything to me besides try to suppress and keep me quiet. Don't worry about me."

She continued, "What you do need to do is find Olivia and make sure she is safe. It is her that they want, and they will never stop until they find her."

"Thank you for your help. Hopefully one day soon we will be safe and I will be sure you are well taken care of," Jack said.

"Jack, perhaps you should take this with you," Betty said. She reached over to a nearby coffee table and grabbed Olivia's box. She gently handed it to Jack.

"Thank you for finding this. It's very special to Olivia," Jack said with a smile.

Jack quickly said goodbye to both Betty and Nick. Their main mission was now accomplished. They had done everything they could. Nick would return to his family in Indianapolis. His family always knew the devious plans Alex and the others were up to, and they would do all they could to stop him. Nick's family had been part of The Resistance for years. When it was known that the Averys were coming to town, Betty knew she had to get Jack's attention. Though she had a few allies inside town, she needed someone who would not be recognized, someone from the outside. Nick was the perfect candidate.

Jack took the fastest route he knew back to his home. Once again he jumped over fences as necessary, not worrying about trespassing on others' property. He wanted to get home to Olivia. He wasn't sure what he was going to do. He knew he had to protect her, if only he could get a hold of his Uncle Frank in Dubuque or someone close by who could help. He didn't know how he was going to leave this town.

He jumped over his backyard fence and landed on his feet this time. He was anxious to see Olivia. Approaching his house, he noticed the back door was slightly open. Pushing it in, he saw things were slightly out of place. He could tell someone had been there since he left. It didn't look to be vandalism, but someone had been in their house looking for something...or maybe someone.

He called out, "Olivia! . . . Olivia! Are you here?" He could hear the thunder outside as he walked through his house. Someone had been walking through the house with muddy shoes. He could tell it wasn't Olivia or Melissa; the size of the footprint was too big. He checked the living room and everything looked to be intact. Going back down the hall, he wanted to check Olivia's room. Looking inside, he found more things out of place. A few of her trinkets on the dresser were knocked over. Her bed was not made. There were a few miscellaneous items on the floor. It made him think of Olivia's shoebox. He held it tightly in his hands.

Looking around the room, he noticed the closet was empty. He walked over and opened the door wider. Olivia's clothes were still hanging up, but the bottom was empty. This was where Olivia stored all her camping gear. It was gone. He remembered seeing her in her room a couple of days ago with all of it out, inspecting it. Jack was actually pleased to see it gone. He hoped Olivia had gathered all her gear together and left before this apparent intruder entered.

He knew he would have to find her. He didn't know exactly where she was going, but he knew she was going to pass through Covington Park. He figured he might be in for a long journey. Jack ran to the kitchen to grab some crackers and a water bottle. He wasn't going to stop until he found Olivia.

In the kitchen, from the corner of his eye, he caught someone lunging toward him. He was holding a gun. Jack reacted quickly, knocking it out of his hand. The man retaliated, throwing Jack to the ground and jumping on top of him. He was a large man, around six feet, three inches tall. He was very overweight. The pressure of his body crushed Jack. The man had an angry look on his face. He was reaching for Jack's throat, trying to choke him. Jack, in a panic, clenched his fist and struck the man directly in the nose. Jack heard something crack. The man let out a sharp scream. Blood poured from his nostrils.

It was obvious the man was not a trained fighter of any sort. Upon noticing the blood, he loosened his grip on Jack, grabbing his nose. Jack kicked the man and lunged for the gun. It had landed under the dining room table about fifteen feet away. Within inches from the gun, the man grabbed Jack's legs and pulled. Jack flipped himself onto his back and kicked the man directly in the nose with the heel of his foot. The man let out another scream and fell onto his back. His head hit hard against the floor. He was out cold.

Jack sat staring at the man on his back. Jack was breathing heavily, full of adrenaline, sweating, and wondering what to do next. For a moment he wondered if he had killed the man. He was relieved to see his stomach moving up and down slightly. He was not dead, just unconscious.

Jack wondered what he should do next. This man was obviously sent to guard the house to see if he or Olivia came back. He wondered if others were coming. He knew he had to find Olivia. He quickly grabbed a small backpack from the front closet. He packed a few small items he thought he would need on an overnight trip. He was also sure to pack a water bottle and the crackers, along with Olivia's box. He thought about taking the man's gun but thought otherwise. If the police were ever called to this scene, he didn't want his fingerprints on it, and, besides, he was basically incompetent as far as handguns were concerned.

Opening the front door, he glanced over his shoulder one more time at the man on his kitchen floor. He was starting to moan. Jack wondered who he was. He wasn't a trained killer. Jack imagined Alex probably roped this man into this job and he didn't know what he was getting himself into. Jack felt sorry for him.

Chapter 16

Jack entered Covington Park. He hoped Olivia was there. If what he read in the library book was correct, he knew she would pass through the park. Where should he begin to look? He thought back to a week ago when he saw Olivia emerge from the woods. He decided to enter at that spot.

The woods were thick. The rain had not let up at all. The moisture in the ground made it difficult for Jack to walk. He was looking frantically for anything that would give him a clue. Where could she be? He remembered that there were caves in these woods. Could she be in one of them? He was starting to get a little anxious, thinking the large man in his house may have awakened and called for help.

For an hour he came up short. He found no trace of Olivia anywhere. He thought that maybe she had already moved on. Just when he was ready to give up, he spotted it. He was on the edge of a hill looking downward on it. It was a small opening under a rock. It was the entrance to a cave. He quickly looked around for the easiest route off the hill to the mouth of the cave.

It was at this moment that he saw her. Olivia emerged from the cave. Her bright red hair was completely soaked. Her hands were muddy from crawling around in the cave. She had on her rain jacket along with her hiking boots. Jack noticed that she was dressed as if she was going on one of their long camping trips. She reached back into the cave and pulled out her camping pack. It was obvious; she was planning to be gone a long time.

Jack was ready to call out to her, when something caught his eye. Someone else was coming out of the cave. He knew who it was, but even then he wondered if his mind was playing tricks on him. He stood staring until the person was completely out of the hole.

It was another little girl, the same height as Olivia and approximately the same age. She also had bright red hair. It was kept the same way as Olivia's. In fact, he wondered if this second girl was Olivia!

Even though he read this in the library, he could barely believe what he was seeing. There were two. He wasn't sure which one was his daughter. He ran down the hill calling out, "Olivia... Olivia!" He didn't worry about traveling down the path, he just ran straight down the hill, through bushes, leaves, and branches. He couldn't get to her fast enough.

The girl dressed in the camping gear yelled out, "Dad!" She ran toward him, dropping her bag along the way. They met at the bottom of the hill and embraced. Jack, overwhelmed, began to cry just a little.

Olivia spoke up, "Dad, we have to hurry, there is no time to lose. They are going to be after us soon. Grandpa is trying to kill us. We must get out of here as soon as we can. Listen, I will explain later, but…"

"Olivia, I know exactly what is going on. I know this town is a secret cult. I know your grandpa is the instigator and master of it all," Jack paused for a moment, "And I know about her," Jack said, nodding toward the other girl.

Olivia wouldn't let him finish. "Dad, this is Jessica, my twin sister," Olivia said, pointing over to the other young girl. "About a week ago, someone helped her escape from a farm house where she was kept. I've been helping her hide this past week. A few people in this town have been panicking, looking for her. Someone has even been watching our house, Daddy!"

Jack had figured this was the case. Since the library, he had been putting everything together; he had read about the history of Singleton and its people. They were descendants of an early Mesopotamian cult from the second century B.C. Alex was in a long line of descendants from the great chief who supposedly received direct revelation from a god. Alex was considered a prophet.

The people's overall beliefs in god and the world were quite complicated and conflicted. Their central figure of evil was the twin. Their beliefs were the origin of the phrase "evil twin." They felt that evil existed in the world and occasionally personified itself in the form of a twin. For the sake of appeasement of the gods and the protection of society, the older twin would be sacrificed on a ceremonial altar.

One of the twins sacrificed was Gus' brother. It was an ongoing secret in the town not to tell Gus. Of course, he was too young to remember; he was a baby when his brother was killed. His parents just told him he had a younger brother who passed away. This wasn't even true because Gus was the younger of the two. When he told Jack about his brother, Melissa panicked and had him fired from his job. She didn't want Jack to have the slightest hint of Singleton's practices.

Now this town was setting its sights on Olivia. Twelve years ago her parents knew they were having twins. Instead of waiting around for one of their little girls to be sacrificed, they ran. They ran from the people of Singleton, and eventually figured the best thing would be to hide Olivia away in a children's home for a few years. Her biological father even secretly worked with one of the nuns to keep her at the children's home as long as possible. Eventually Olivia was found. Alex sent his own daughter, Melissa, on a mission to adopt this girl from the home. It was true that Jack and Melissa's marriage had been a sham since the beginning. Melissa merely used him to get Olivia. Adoption was always an easier process to a two-parent family.

Jessica had a similar story. She was put in the foster system in Texas, where she was passed from home to home for a few years. At the age of five, she was found and recovered by the people of Singleton. Alex spared no expense at keeping the rituals of Singleton alive. The town must be cleansed from the evil that came out of it. Nothing would stop him.

Jack realized they better keep moving. "All right, girls, we need to get going. They might be here soon." Instantly Jack started treating Jessica like his own daughter, like he had known her for years. He immediately accepted and loved her. He knew she needed protection too. He was going to get them both out of Singleton.

They traveled for about half an hour. Jack noticed that Jessica was not used to hiking through the woods. She wasn't dressed for hiking either. She stumbled often, and had to stop and take breaks because the trip was very strenuous for her. Jack tried carrying her on his back for a while, but this definitely slowed the pace. He was worried. The town was probably realizing what was transpiring, and at the pace he and the girls were going they would probably be caught soon. He wondered where to go. He knew that Melissa knew where all his relatives lived, so hiding out there would be futile. In fact, Jack realized that hiding anywhere was useless because Alex was never going to stop looking for him or the girls. What was he to do?

♋

City Hall was filled. Alex had called an emergency special meeting for the town. He knew what was happening. He was both angry and upset. Jack had left his house without being immediately noticed. Alex had hired a special watchman to keep an eye on the house. His name was Hibbert. Luckily for Jack, Hibbert sat out front of Jack's house in his car and didn't see him as he left his house to run after Nick. Olivia also had sense enough to escape out the back of the house in order not to be seen. Eventually when Hibbert didn't see any movement in the house for a while, he decided to take matters into his own hands and break in. It was just a few minutes later that he heard Jack come through the back door of the house. In a panic, he tried to attack Jack, but that ended badly for him. Just before this special city meeting, Hibbert awoke from his unconscious state. He confessed to Alex what had transpired. This gave the meeting a greater sense of urgency.

Alex had called this special meeting to set things in motion. The whole town showed up, and he stood before them on a stage behind a podium. The ceremonial sacrifice was supposed to take place in a few weeks. They were waiting for the middle of September, their religious New Year for the town. Alex figured that now Jack and Olivia would have to be kept in confinement until the appropriate day.

"Men and women of Singleton!" Alex started the meeting, "Our plans have been foiled and our sacrificial lamb has run away." The people reacted with groans. He continued, "It appears that Jack, along with our lamb, is probably fleeing to Peoria or possibly Dubuque, where he has relatives. We must not let them escape. For tonight, I'm going to need everyone to spread out around the town and search every area of it! We will stop at nothing to find them."

A man shouted at Alex from the back of the hall, "What about your mother? You know she's behind all of this. She is going to ruin it all."

Alex shot back, "I will deal with her in time. Don't worry about her." Their culture held matriarchs in such a high regard that there was nothing substantive Alex could do to stop her. She would always have her allies and as long as she was alive she would cause disruption.

At that moment the doors of city hall creaked open. Alex looked to the back of the hall to see Henry entering. He was dressed like a farmer in overalls, work boots, and an old baseball cap on his head. He looked sad and worried. He did not want to face Alex.

For the moment Alex was at a loss. Everyone's eyes were fixed on Henry for he was rarely seen in town, and the people were wondering why he was here. Alex spoke to him, "Henry Jacobson, is everything well with you?"

He took off his cap and held it in his hands, revealing his bald head. "Well, no sir. You see, someone has taken the girl, Jessica."

The people of town were a little confused as many of them didn't know that Jessica was being kept in his basement. Alex had put her there because he did not want Jack or Olivia somehow seeing her before the sacrifice of Olivia.

Alex spoke up, clearly angry, "What? How could you let this happen? Henry, when did this occur?"

Henry was sweating profusely at this point. "About a week ago," he responded hesitantly.

Alex was filled with anger. Why had he not been told? He shot back, condemning the farmer, "If the sacrifice is missed, the blood and curse of this town will be on your hands."

Betty had a few allies working undercover in town. They learned the whereabouts of Jessica. With her nephew's help, she orchestrated a plan to break into Henry's home and take the girl. Though she was not going to be sacrificed, Betty took it upon herself to have her rescued as well. She knew that the very presence of Jessica would also help confirm the validity of her story to Jack. After being rescued, she was hid away in one of the obscure caves in Covington Park. Nick would come by daily to make sure all was well with her and that she had enough food. Last Sunday she was getting just a bit of fresh air when Olivia spotted her climbing out of the cave. Jessica explained to her about Singleton and the danger she was in. For the past week, they had met often and were preparing themselves for their current escape.

Alex continued with the meeting. He organized the people into groups with which the whole town could be adequately searched. "I will lead a special search party through the east woods. Stewart will bring a team and search through Covington. Everyone else search every corner of this town, including my mother's house. Do whatever it takes to find those girls. They are the key to our town's safety. We must appease the gods. The sacrifice is demanded."

Everyone was ready to leave when a man in the front asked, "What about Jack? What if we find him?"

"Kill him on site!" responded a familiar voice. Alex turned to see his daughter, smiling as she said it. She was finally ready to put an end to Jack Avery. She hated him.

᥿

Alex and a company of thirty approached the east woods. Melissa was with him. This was the area of the supposed Font Lake, but Alex and Melissa both knew there was no lake inside. Using all his resources Alex fooled every map producer into thinking there was a small lake located in middle of these woods. Melissa figured that Jack would probably travel northeast, knowing there were more wooded areas going that direction. Jack and Olivia had enough backpacking skills to probably make it to Indianapolis.

They approached the fence outlying the woods. Alex could tell someone had entered. The main gate's lock had been cut and the gate was swung open. Hopefully this meant Jack and the girls were inside. "After you," he said quietly to his daughter.

"Thank you, Father," Melissa said, passing through the gate, followed by Alex and the others. Since they left city hall, Melissa could think of nothing but how much she hated Jack. After marrying him, she regretted picking him to be the one to help her find and adopt Olivia. She was hoping he was going to be a man she could force to do whatever she wanted. She thought her pure beauty was enough to subject him to her will. Melissa had been constantly disappointed when Jack would challenge her or seek to lead their family. She hated Jack! And the fact that Olivia attached herself to him made it even worse.

There was a slight murmur in the crowd as most had never been in this restricted area except during the ceremonies. Some were excited, others were frightened. A few were carrying torches to light the way, similar to a witch hunt a hundred years old. A small portion of the town had always been uncomfortable with the history and religious beliefs of Singleton. More would have liked to join The Resistance but were too afraid of Alex and the others in town.

About a hundred yards into the woods, they came to a clearing. Trees and shrubs were cleared in an area of about a thirty yard diameter. The grass was well kept. Cult symbols were painted on stones around the outskirts of the perimeter. Someone in town was responsible for taking care of this area.

In the middle of the clearing there was an altar. It sat about five feet in height. It was mostly gold plated with various hieroglyphics and other symbols painted on the outside of the structure. It was the place where the sacrifice of twins would take place. It was supposedly the same altar as was used two thousand years ago, just repaired and updated through the years. It was a very sacred sight for the people of Singleton. It was not to be touched.

Entering the area, Alex was the first to see the odd sight. On top of the altar sat a man, relaxed, smoking a cigar. He had his back turned to the crowd, looking off into the distance and up at the stars. He definitely heard the crowd blazing through the woods, but chose not to let it bother him. Alex, on the hand, was extremely angry, but kept his cool.

Melissa shuffled to the front of the crowd to see what was going on. She recognized the man right away and lashed out in anger, "Jack Avery! What are you doing? Get off our altar now!"

Jack looked over his shoulder and took a small puff on his cigar. Giving her a small smile, he responded "Hey darlin', how are you?"

Chapter 17

A large man in the crowd walked over to where Jack was sitting, grabbed him by the back of the head and threw him off the altar. His cigar went flying. Jack hit the ground and rolled a few feet. The man stopped him by placing his foot in the center of Jack's chest. Jack pushed the man's foot to the side and stood up. Brushing himself off, he faced Alex and the crowd.

"Well, Jack, I guess you found our altar." Alex said, pushing his long grey hair behind his ears.

"It's quite lovely, Alex, and it reminds me of you: sick, twisted, and at its core utterly meaningless." Jack had been sitting on the altar for close to two hours, waiting to be found. He had lots of time to think about what he was going to say to his wife and father-in-law. He now had no fear of them and wanted them to know it.

"Jack, must we continue with these insults? I will not play games with you anymore. You know what I want, and we must have her to appease the gods."

"Alex, I read your books in the library, and I know you are a sick, sick man. You are deceiving these people with your faulty religion." A hush fell over the crowd. The people in the crowd were shocked by this statement. They had a real true reverence of Alex and thought of him as close to a deity.

Melissa in her anger spoke up from the crowd, "Jack, you have always messed things up. You are a pathetic man, and if you'd had half a brain, I would've at least tried to explain to you the traditions and beliefs of Singleton." Jack thought she looked so very evil in the glow of the torches. He wondered how he ever had found her attractive. He was done with Melissa and he didn't even want to respond to her statement. He just ignored her.

Alex pulled Jack to the side with their backs toward the crowd. He spoke softly to Jack, "Listen, Jack, before this gets out of hand, I want you to know there is nothing personal intended by this. I think you understand by now that we need the oldest twin for our sacrifice. It would be best if you just told us where she was, instead of all this running and chasing we've been doing. It needs to end tonight."

"She's gone!" Jack said loudly, "I sent her and her sister on their way. More than anyone I know, Olivia is skilled in the woods. She knows how to survive and she knows how to hide. You won't be able to track her."

"Jack, you can't be serious. I found her once and we will find her again. The people of Singleton let me use their money at my disposal. If you haven't figured it out, I have the ability to manipulate maps and destroy cell phone towers. There is nothing I can't do. I have an unlimited amount of resources. I may not be able to track her now, but I will eventually find her. You cannot stop me, Jack. I'm sorry."

"I know I can't. I'm not going to." Jack said, looking straight into Alex's eyes.

"What?"

"You heard me. I read all about you in the library. I know the history of this place. I know what you are capable of. I had to come to the realization that there is nothing I could do to stop you."

Alex looked puzzled. "Then why are you here, Jack? Why didn't you escape with the girls?"

"I want to make a deal with you."

Alex laughed a little. "Jack, maybe you are as stupid as Melissa says. You can't pay me off. I have more money than you will ever have." He began to walk away toward the crowd.

Jack shouted out, "Take me instead!"

Alex turned to face Jack. He was close to the others. Melissa's eyes grew large; she knew what he was talking about. He continued, "Yes, take me instead."

"Jack, you can't be serious," Alex said in frustration, "You read our books. You know the significance behind our rituals and sacrifices. Only a twin will appease the gods."

"He is a twin," Melissa said under her breath. Alex turned to face her. He was shocked, surprised she never told him.

Jack continued, "She's right, Alex. My younger brother Steve is my identical twin."

"He's telling the truth," Melissa said looking at her father. Alex didn't know what to say. Nothing like this had ever been done in their history. He wondered if this would be acceptable. Jack could tell that Alex was not convinced of this plan. He needed to do a little convincing and persuading.

Feeling like he was now in control, Jack pulled Alex aside, away from the crowd and spoke softly. The crowd could not hear, "Alex, take me instead. Let Olivia live."

"Nice try, Jack, but I don't think the people of this town would find that as an acceptable alternative. We can only accept those born or conceived here."

"Alex, think about it this way. I read in the history of this town that the people were repulsed when Gus' brother was killed. Many of the people rebelled, including your own mother. That is how The Resistance began. People do not want to see another young one killed. It will turn the people against you. Take me instead, and promise you will stop chasing Olivia."

Alex looked away from Jack, knowing he had a point, but unsure about what to do. He thought out loud, "I just don't know. Nothing like this has ever been done before. I don't know how the people will respond."

Jack decided he needed to go for his heart. He had another card up his sleeve, "Alex, I also know about your wife that you loved so much. I know about twenty-five years ago, a few days after a ceremonial sacrifice, she took her own life. She couldn't live with herself after the sacrifice of a small boy. You loved her!"

Alex did not respond. He was angry. He was angry at his daughter for choosing him. He was angry at Jack for bringing up his wife. He was angry because he knew he was right.

Jack continued, "Listen, Alex, take me instead of Olivia. As sick and twisted as this ritual is, at least for mercy's sake, do not bring another child into this."

Alex seemed to look off in the far distance, thinking about what Jack just proposed. Jack then continued in a whisper, "Alex, I'm going to shoot straight with you. You don't believe all this, do you?"

"Jack, what are you talking about? Don't be crazy!"

"Alex, come on, be honest with me. These people are following you like zombies. They are willing to lay down their lives for you. You have all their money at your disposal. Your ancestors might have believed it, but you don't care about all this religious garbage. You can twist things however you like. Tell them I'm an acceptable sacrifice. Make it work somehow! You know you just care about the money."

Alex thought for a moment and then gave Jack a small smile, "You forgot about the power, Jack. The money is great, but it is wonderful having people at my disposal. They will give me anything, including their lives."

"Then make it happen, Alex. Let Olivia live in peace, take me instead."

Alex looked back at the people and thought about the proposal. After about a minute he looked back at Jack and spoke, "Ok, I will make it happen. You must play along if this is going to work." He began to walk back to the crowd.

Jack shouted, "Promise me this—that Olivia and her sister are going to be left alone! They will be safe!"

Alex turned to face him, "You have my word, Jack. Nothing will happen to them."

Jack felt at ease, even though he knew what would happen in the next couple of weeks. As evil as Alex was, Jack felt that this promise would at least be held up. A couple of men in the crowd came forward and arrested Jack. He would be kept in a secret prison before he would be sacrificed. He didn't want to die, but he was thankful that Olivia was going to be safe.

Now that the storm had passed, it was a clear night. He looked up at the stars one more time. Jack thought about Olivia and all the nights they had camped together. He started to tear up. He mumbled a little prayer, "Thank you, God, for the time I got to have with her. She blessed my life so much. Thank you for letting me choose her." A large man came from the crowd and placed a black hood over Jack's head. He saw the stars no more.

♋

Olivia and Jessica fought through the woods. They headed toward Chicago. They had already made it four miles since leaving Jack. Both girls had been crying ever since they left him. He had talked with them at length about what was going to happen. There was always hope that they could reach the authorities in time for them to intervene in the sacrifice, but Olivia felt in her heart of hearts that she would never see him again. It was very heartbreaking, but she knew she had to stay strong for her sister.

The plan was for the girls to travel to the outskirts of Chicago. Alex had associates all around the area. The girls didn't want to be seen or discovered by any of Alex's allies. Just in case Alex didn't agree to stop chasing them, Jack thought they had better reach the Chicago area before calling for help.

Olivia had packed enough dry food and backpacking meals in order for them to make it. Over the past couple of years she had learned all the necessary skills for backpacking long distances, including how to start a fire. Once near Chicago, Olivia would get in touch with her great Uncle Frank in Dubuque, who would come for them. Jack had given her his wallet which had in it at least eighty dollars in cash, along with credit cards if they got into a pinch. Olivia knew she had everything physically to make the trip, but the emotional struggle of losing her father was what made it terribly difficult.

Jessica tripped on a log. She landed in some thorns and let out a sharp scream. Olivia stopped. She turned to help her sister up; Olivia noticed that she was crying. Jessica was slow to get up and she was bleeding slightly. Olivia quickly got out her first aid kit and cleaned Jessica's small wounds.

"We must keep going, Jess. We don't know if they are going to take Daddy's offer. They could be on us at any moment." Jessica remained silent, wiping her face of the tears in her eyes. Olivia applied two band-aids and repacked the kit.

Olivia tried to stay strong, "We need to keep quiet and stay in the shadows. If we can make it to the river, we will be safe for now."

Jessica, looking out in the distance, spoke through her tears, "I just can't believe he took your place. I can't believe he would do that for you."

Olivia spoke with strength, "Listen, Jessica, I'm sorry you only knew him for a short while. He's a wonderful dad. He was always there for me and made whatever sacrifice he needed to make. This is no different. He's the best dad ever."

The girls got up and went on their way. It was getting late into the evening, but their adrenaline was going strong and neither suggested sleep. They wanted to get as far from Singleton as possible. They knew they weren't going to be completely safe until they made it to the Chicago area.

After traveling for another twenty minutes, they came across an open field. It looked to be an area where cows or some other animals grazed. Their plan was to avoid these open areas. They would try to stay in wooded sections or hide away in corn fields as much as possible. Because it was Illinois, they knew they would have to pass through some open fields. Their plan was to run across these areas as fast as possible in order not to be seen. This current field was about a half-mile across to the other tree line. There was no way around it, so they decided to quickly hurry across.

Both girls ran out into the middle of the field. It was here that Olivia stopped briefly to look up at the stars. She noticed it was a clear night. The clouds had passed from the earlier storm and the stars were bright. It was a beautiful night. She was caught up in the moment and her worries left her.

She thought back to their last backpacking trip outside of Colorado Springs. She remembered the wonderful time she and her father had together, quietly looking up at the stars, thinking about life. The memory seemed so vivid at the moment. It seemed like only yesterday. She began to think of her father and how much he cared for her. Somehow she knew that he was looking up at the same stars at that moment. She loved him so much and thanked God for her father's love.

Epilogue

Olivia and Jessica looked over their father's grave. Yes, they both thought of him as their father. He had given his life for their freedom and safety. Even though Jessica had only interacted with him for about an hour, she felt as if she knew him deeply. She was never very close to her adopted parents as both were residents of Singleton who adopted her simply for Alex's mission. Over the years Olivia talked about her father constantly, telling Jessica stories about what a great man he was.

It had been ten years since the night they left him. They made it safely to Yorkville, outside of Chicago. It took them twelve days of rigorous hiking. Upon arriving they called Olivia's uncle Frank in Dubuque, who quickly came and stayed with them in Chicago.

It took a long time to convince Uncle Frank of the conspiracy going on in Singleton. Eventually the authorities were contacted and Singleton was investigated. Upon the story breaking in local newspapers, various people around the area of western Illinois came forward, expressing their concerns and rumors they heard about the town. The most outspoken person was the old man Olivia met at the gas station just before arriving in Singleton. He had always known that the town was up to no good, but he knew that no one would listen to an old man with a conspiracy theory. The investigation gave him an open door to report his information to the authorities.

Sadly, Alex moved up the date of the sacrifice. Jack was killed just a two days after the girls left. He knew the girls would go right to the police and he needed time to create a good alibi. The people of Singleton had been trained at constructing alibis. They had been doing it for two thousand years. Thankfully, The Resistance had grown strong enough to counteract what the residents said to the police. This time the people of Singleton didn't get away with it. The town was exposed.

Olivia and Jessica became household names. When it was confirmed that the charges against the town were true, it became the number one news story on every network. Documentaries were done on the history of the town and what they believed. It was emphasized how *Singletons,* as they were called, did not like twins. Olivia and Jessica did countless interviews and Olivia's memoirs became a number one best seller.

Many of the people in Singleton were arrested and a few of the buildings became museums to commemorate what happened with the Avery family. Melissa was arrested and received life in prison. Alex, seeing how everything was unfolding, fled the scene weeks before everything broke loose. He was never found. Many people have a theory that he is hiding somewhere in Europe.

Betty gained great fame as well. She moved outside of Singleton to Indianapolis where she lived the rest of her days near Nick's family. She passed away a few years ago. Her funeral was televised.

Through it all, Olivia just wanted her father back. She and Jessica lived with their uncle Steve in Denver. Both girls were homeschooled through high school and also attended college in the area. For the first few years they endured hours upon hours of counseling and family therapy. They were also constantly harassed by the paparazzi and had to have special bodyguards escort them whenever they went into town. Even though things were familiar to Olivia in Denver, they were never the same without her father.

The wind began to blow slightly as they looked over the grave. Both girls began to cry. Jessica grabbed Olivia's hand to comfort her. This was the first time they had been to his grave in Western Illinois, just outside of Singleton. Olivia said a little prayer. She spoke quietly, "Thank you for your sacrifice, thank you for taking my place." Truly greater love has no one than this, that he lay down his life for the ones he loves. Unlike Alex, Jack understood the true meaning of sacrifice.

ABOUT THE AUTHOR . . .

Tony Myers is a fiction author and speaker. He enjoys looking for creative ways and illustrations to communicate truth. He and his wife, Charity, have two kids and currently live in Waterloo, Iowa. He can be contacted through his website: www.tonymyers.net or through twitter: @tony1myers

Also, check out Tony Myers' other books, *Stealing the Magic* and *The Beauty of a Beast.*

Stealing the Magic

"Myers delivers a page-turning mystery that grips the reader with its relatable characters and compelling plot. A taut, satisfying story for young suspense lovers and seasoned readers alike."

- Pamela Crane, literary judge and author of the award-winning *A Secondhand Life*

The Beauty of a Beast

"Nothing captivates an audience of all ages like nights, princesses, dragons, beasts and courage. The Beauty of a Beast proves that true. It is one of those books with a very familiar plot line, but an extreme twist at the end. While reading it, I was on the edge of my seat. Tony Myers does a fantastic job of capturing his audience's attention and not letting it go till the end of the book. Each character comes alive with every paragraph as their world becomes as real as ours. This clean, mind-blowing, nail-biting, easy-to-read book will have you eagerly turning each page and then anxiously anticipating the next book!"

- Aaron Moore

Made in the USA
Monee, IL
04 March 2020